Frankie put her nose to the ground.

The K-9 moved in circles and paced back and forth, but then she trotted in a straight line as if she'd picked up on something.

Lydia followed and they came to a no-trespassing sign. River commanded Frankie to stop.

"This is private land," he said. "We need to get permission from the owner to go on it."

"Did she pick up on a scent?" Lydia asked.

"She did, but she never alerted. Maybe whoever owns this land saw something."

A sharp crack penetrated the air. Frankie let out a bark as River pulled Lydia to the ground.

"We're being shot at." He grabbed his gun. "We need to get back to the car...and get out of here!"

* * *

COLORADO K-9 UNIT

Searching for the Truth by Laura Scott
Tracking the Taken Child by Sharon Dunn
Danger in the Rockies by Terri Reed
Protecting the Baby by Jodie Bailey
Fugitive Manhunt by Sharee Stover
Hunting an Arsonist by Jessica R. Patch
Uncovering Explosive Secrets by Maggie K. Black
Unraveling a Crime Ring by Valerie Hansen
Christmas K-9 Security by Lynette Eason & Lenora Worth

Ever since she found the Nancy Drew books with the pink covers in the country school library, **Sharon Dunn** has loved mystery and suspense. In 2014, she lost her beloved husband of nearly twenty-seven years to cancer. She has three grown children. When she is not writing, she enjoys reading, sewing and walks. She loves to hear from readers. You can contact her via her website at sharondunnbooks.net.

Books by Sharon Dunn

Love Inspired Suspense

Mountain Captive
Undercover Threat
Alaskan Christmas Target
Undercover Mountain Pursuit
Crime Scene Cover-Up
Christmas Hostage
Montana Cold Case Conspiracy
Montana Witness Chase
Kidnapped in Montana
Defending the Child
Targeted Montana Witness
Montana Ranch Crime Ring

Mountain Country K-9 Unit

Tracing a Killer

Dakota K-9 Unit

Double Protection Duty

Colorado K-9 Unit

Tracking the Taken Child

Visit the Author Profile page at LoveInspired.com for more titles.

TRACKING THE TAKEN CHILD

SHARON DUNN

Special thanks and acknowledgment are given to Sharon Dunn for her contribution to the Colorado K-9 Unit miniseries.

Recycling programs for this product may not exist in your area.

ISBN-13: 978-1-335-95769-6

Tracking the Taken Child

For questions and comments about the quality of this book, please contact us at CustomerService@Harlequin.com.

Love Inspired
22 Adelaide St. West, 41st Floor
Toronto, Ontario M5H 4E3, Canada
www.LoveInspired.com

HarperCollins Publishers
Macken House, 39/40 Mayor Street Upper,
Dublin 1, D01 C9W8, Ireland
www.HarperCollins.com

Printed in Lithuania

For, lo, the winter is past, the rain is over and gone;
the flowers appear on the earth; the time of the
singing of birds is come.

—*Song of Solomon* 2:11–12

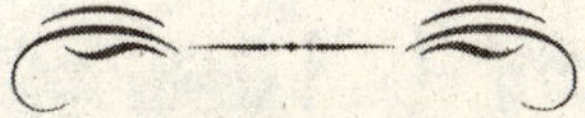

For my mother, Mary Ellen, who loved nature.
Always, there is sorrow that you didn't live to
see your grandchildren or know that
I succeeded as a writer. I think of you often.

ONE

Panic sliced through preschool teacher Lydia Caldwell's awareness when she turned to find that her three-year-old daughter Elsie had disappeared. Ruthie, Elsie's hiking buddy, sat alone, munching on a peanut butter sandwich. The other ten children were paired up and resting beside the Peewee Trail they were hiking as a class. Just moments before, they'd sat down to eat lunch. Lydia had turned away from her daughter only for a second to help Benson with his juice box.

"Where did Elsie go?" Lydia looked at her daughter's hiking buddy.

Ruthie set her sandwich down and pointed behind her at the trees that were just off the trail. "She saw a butterfly, Miss Caldwell."

Lydia's co-teacher, Angel, a tall woman in her early twenties with round brown eyes and short black hair, gestured that Lydia should go. "We've got this. Go find her."

The other eleven children would be fine with Angel and the volunteer parent, a kind father of twins.

"She's such a nature lover," said Lydia, trying to sound casual as she headed toward the trees. A familiar tension coiled through her chest and stomach. When her child was out of eyesight, maternal instinct kicked in. Elsie was probably fine. How far could she get in less than a minute? Pretty far actually, the three-year-old could run like the wind.

Shaking off the rising fear, Lydia pushed through the trees, calling Elsie's name. Relief spread through her when she saw Elsie's pink-sequined baseball hat and floral windbreaker. Her daughter turned toward her, placing her finger perpendicular to her lips.

The little girl pointed to a cluster of flowers on the ground where a butterfly flexed its wings. Warmth washed over Lydia when she realized the sacredness of the moment she'd stepped into. To chase a butterfly with her daughter was not an event to be missed.

The butterfly lifted and flew in the direction of another cluster of flowers. Stepping softly, Lydia caught up with Elsie, who reached for her mother's hand as they moved in unison toward the butterfly. Elsie's green eyes were wide with wonder. Her daughter had inherited her eye color but not her auburn hair. Elsie's strawberry-blond hair was from her father's side of the family.

Though her divorce from her husband was a little over a year old, it still stung. When they'd first met, Sloane had appeared to be everything she'd wanted in a husband, but shortly after they were married, she realized he had a drinking problem he'd hidden from her when they were dating. The drinking got worse after Elsie's birth. The final straw had been when he'd driven under the influence with Elsie in the car.

As much as she hadn't wanted a divorce, she wasn't about to risk her child's life to keep her marriage together. Now it was just the two of them, though Sloane's parents remained involved in Elsie's life. Lydia had no other family. She'd been orphaned at a young age and raised by an efficient but cold aunt who'd recently died.

The butterfly alighted again, and they moved deeper into the woods until the trees opened up into a meadow.

Relishing the warmth of the little hand she held in her own, Lydia scanned the area, looking for the orange wings.

Elsie pointed at the sky, and they hurried to catch up with their flying companion. They came to the edge of a rocky area with a steep drop-off.

Elsie jumped up and down and opened and closed her hands while she looked up. "Goodbye, Mister Butterfly."

"Thanks for the adventure. Mister Butterfly," said Lydia to the sky though she could no longer see the insect.

"Do you think he will go all the way across these mountains, Mommy?" Elsie grabbed her mother's hand and swung it back and forth.

"Probably. Who knows where his journey will take him?" Peering down at the near vertical incline made her lightheaded. Lydia took a step back and guided Elsie away from the ledge as well.

Elsie tilted her head, a smile gracing her lips and bringing light to her eyes. "I think he's going to fly all the way up to God." She lifted her arms dramatically and then let them fall at her sides.

"Maybe so."

Elsie twisted her body back and forth as her gaze fell to the ground a few feet away. "Look, yellow flowers." She ran the short distance to the flowers Lydia had always called buttercups.

Lydia glanced out at the giant expanse of canyon, thinking about the butterfly. Almost from the day she was born, Elsie had a connection with animals and nature. They needed to get back with the rest of the class, but this moment had been so worth the detour. She took in a deep gratitude-filled breath.

Heavy footsteps pounded behind her.

Before she could turn, a force hit Lydia's back. She stumbled forward, her feet hovering on the edge of the drop-off, arms flapping. Another blow sent her down the steep incline. She screamed.

"Momeeeeeeee—"

Her daughter's voice seemed to get cut off.

Lydia somersaulted through the air, her arms and legs crashing against rock. She rolled several more feet before coming to a stop on a narrow ledge. Blue sky filled her field of vision. She struggled for a deep breath, not moving as the rocks and brush above seemed to gyrate. The fall had knocked the wind out of her and made her dizzy.

Someone had pushed her. She could've died. Her heart raced as pain shot through her back and legs when she sat up. She'd fallen at least twenty feet. Her first thought was of her daughter.

"Elsie?"

She stared, hoping and praying to see Elsie's bright face leaning over the edge. Nothing. Elsie would've come to the edge if she could have. A dark thought hovered at the corners of her brain. No, she would not let herself go there. Maybe her child had run for help. But what about the person who'd pushed her? What was going on?

Gripping the protruding rocks, she pulled herself upright, feeling pain in her arms with every movement. Nothing was broken, but she was pretty bruised and scratched up. She got to her feet on the narrow ledge and shouted, "Somebody, help."

Only the wind answered back.

She found her first foothold and, with some effort, climbed up a few feet. She called for help again and then reached for another protruding rock. Her mind was starting to process what had happened. If she hadn't landed on the narrow ledge, she could have fallen all the way to the bottom. She pulled herself up closer to the top until she could peer over. Her breath caught. No Elsie.

"Help, someone." Her voice sounded weak as panic set in.

She climbed the remaining distance. Before she even got to her feet, she saw the scattered yellow flowers and the pink hat lying on the ground. It felt as though an anvil had been placed on her chest. A deep breath was impossible.

The parent volunteer, a short, bald man, emerged through the trees.

Lydia ran toward him, stopping to pick up the pink cap. "Did Elsie come back to the group?"

"No." He shook his head, sunlight reflecting off his glasses. "We were starting to worry about you two. The others are done with their lunch. I was sent to find you."

Her hands trembled as her voice cracked. "You didn't see Elsie?"

The father must have seen the terror in Lydia's eyes. He gripped Lydia's wrist. "Is everything all right?"

Lydia felt as though she were pulling words up from the bottom of her feet. "Call search and rescue. I think my daughter is missing." She could not bring herself to say what might have really happened. That Elsie had been kidnapped.

K-9 Officer River Jameson listened as the call came through his radio.

"Suspected missing child near the Peewee Trail on Ridge Mountain. Foul play highly likely."

His stomach tied in knots as he absorbed the words of the conversation between search and rescue and the 911 operator. A missing child rarely had a positive outcome. He of all people knew that, after his last case involving a child had come to a harrowing end.

Though he had been on a mission for the task force he was part of, trying to uncover a baby adoption ring that was targeting young vulnerable mothers in the area, he wasn't far from where the girl had been reported missing. He and his K-9, a female yellow Lab named Frankie, were close and they could help. He had to help… After his last case, he couldn't stand by if an innocent was at risk. The task force assignment could wait.

The sign came up for the hiking trails on Ridge Mountain, and he hit his blinker. He pulled out his radio and spoke into it. "This is Officer Jameson of Ridge PD. I'm close to the sight and have my search and rescue dog with me."

The operator responded. "The volunteer team won't arrive for another twenty minutes. And some other K-9 officers are on the way as well. We could use all the help we can get."

Time was of the essence in finding this girl. "I got this." He turned his head slightly and addressed his next comment to the yellow Lab in the backseat kennel. "You ready to go to work, Frankie?"

Frankie responded with an enthusiastic bark.

As he drove toward the trailhead parking lot that connected to where the child had disappeared, River's thoughts turned to the task force and another life that needed saving. Mia Andrews, a pregnant missing teen from Denver. Her grandfather, Dodger, was a philanthropist known throughout the state for his funding of K-9 operations, and he'd been instrumental in forming the Colorado K-9 Unit, which comprised K-9 officers from across the state, to find his granddaughter. The task force was also determined to get justice for three other young women, all pregnant and in their late teens, who'd disappeared over the past year. Unfortunately, the three teens had been murdered and their babies had been taken. The COK9 team believed they were dealing with a ruthless illegal adoption ring operating around the Denver area. If they didn't act fast, Mia Andrews would be their next victim. The clock was ticking. Mia would only be kept alive until she gave birth in October. It was May, and River hoped they found her well before it was too late.

His task today was to interview a colleague of another murder victim, Gayle Gorman, who was from Ridge, where River worked as a local police officer when not with the task force. Gayle Gorman's body had been found by hikers in a remote area outside of Ridge. But recently her colleague, who'd worked with her at Ridge Burgers and More, had come forward saying she had information. Hopefully there was a new lead. He just needed to show up for the interview at the burger place before Gayle's former work colleague went off shift at 7:00 p.m. In the meantime, he'd help search for the missing toddler.

He pulled into the parking lot beside a small bus that said Great Beginnings Preschool.

A short way up the trail, he could see a group of children with two adults: a man and a woman. He opened Frankie's kennel and gave the command to dismount. The yellow Lab looked up at him in expectation.

One of the adults, a young woman with black hair, came toward him. "You're search and rescue?"

"Yes." It appeared that he was the first on the scene.

"Elsie's mom is looking for her. Mr. Crane and I had to stay with the other children. We need to get them loaded into the bus and calmed down. They're all worried about Elsie."

"More search and rescue people are on the way, but I need to start ASAP." He didn't want to say it, but the forest was filled with hazards for such a young child even if there wasn't foul play.

The young woman held up a pink baseball cap. "This belonged to the little girl. Lydia, her mom, knew you would need it to get a scent off of."

He took the hat. That the distraught mom had had the presence of mind to know what would be needed to find her child spoke volumes about Lydia's composure in what was one of the most difficult challenges a parent could face. "Which direction did the child go when you last saw her?"

The dark-haired woman pointed toward the trees by the trail. "Lydia can tell you more about what happened."

He held the baseball hat toward Frankie's nose. She sniffed and gave a tail wag. He handed the cap back to her. "The other searchers will need that when they arrive."

He took Frankie off her leash. "Frankie, find." The yellow Lab headed up the trail. Right before he left, River glanced down at the parking lot. On the mountain road below, he saw two other vehicles headed up. He'd have help soon enough.

Tail moving, nose to the ground, Frankie was on the scent. The trail was hot right now. Gray clouds overhead suggested that rain was coming, which would muddy the scent for the dogs. They needed to find this kid fast.

When he entered the trees, he heard a woman's voice frantically calling, "Elsie. Elsie, where are you?"

A petite redheaded woman emerged from a different part of the forest. He'd seen that pale skin and stricken expression before on other parents.

His mind whirled back to eight months ago and the case that still haunted him. A five-year-old boy had seemingly wandered away from the family farm. River and Frankie had been called in with other search and rescue personnel. They had searched in wider and wider circles around the farm. An offhanded remark by a neighbor helping with the search made him realize that the child hadn't wandered away but had been taken by a noncustodial parent. By the time they'd located the father and son, it was too late. The man had been driving too fast and shot through a guardrail. Noah hadn't survived. Why hadn't he asked more questions up front? The search would have been conducted differently, and Noah might still be alive. Search and rescue often didn't have positive outcomes, but losing Noah was the first time a child had died on his watch.

Though Noah's mother had been standing in a cluster of people that day, he'd recognized her even at a distance just by the look on her face. Regret twisted through his stomach. He vowed that this time things would be different. He wouldn't assume, he'd ask more questions.

He ran toward the redheaded woman. Her green eyes looked as though a veil had been pulled over them.

"You're Elsie's mother?"

She nodded.

He held out his hand to her. "I'm Officer River Jameson and this is my partner, Frankie. Can you tell me what happened? Where did you last see your daughter?"

She pointed toward a meadow that led to a canyon. "We were…chasing a butterfly." Her eyes glazed over.

"The call said there was foul play?"

She looked right at him as she shook her head. "Someone pushed me…and I fell." Again, she indicated the canyon, which must have a steep incline.

Had someone intended to kill Lydia or just get her out of the way so they could snatch little Elsie? He scanned the trees as his hand flexed toward his holstered gun. What if the perpetrator was still around? There'd been two other cars besides the bus in the parking lot.

Lydia was in rough shape, but he needed to ask questions in order to understand what had happened.

"You didn't see who pushed you?"

She shook her head. "When I climbed back up, Elsie was… Elsie was…gone." She drew her hand to her trembling mouth as tears flowed.

He reached out to squeeze her arm as a show of support.

His mind raced. A possible kidnapping. But how could they have gotten away? The kidnapper wouldn't be able to get back to one of the cars in the parking lot. He or she might still be in the forest, waiting for a chance to escape.

He could hear the baying of a hound and the barking of another dog growing louder.

"Mrs.—"

"It's Miss Caldwell. It used to be Mrs."

He sensed deep pain behind that bit of information. "Miss Caldwell. We've got more dogs on the scent, why don't you go back to trailhead and wait?" She would be safer with people around. If there had been one attempt on her life, there could be another.

She gripped his arm as her eyes cleared. "No, thank you. I will look for my daughter."

The quiver had left her voice, and he saw that look of steel resolve in her features.

She pulled her phone out. "This is her. This is my Elsie."

He stared at a smiling green-eyed child with teeth like little pearls and a bright expression.

"I'll follow you. If—when we find Elsie, I don't want her to be afraid because you're a stranger. Though I think she would totally gravitate toward your dog. Elsie loves animals…" Her voice trailed off, and she got that faraway look in her eyes again.

The reasoning wasn't unsound. She'd be safe if she

stayed close to him. “All right, Miss Caldwell, let’s find your daughter.”

It appeared they were dealing with an abduction. Elsie hadn’t just wandered away and gotten lost. Maybe the kidnappers hadn’t escaped the wilderness.

The clock was ticking to find the little girl alive. He prayed that they weren’t already too late.

TWO

Rain sprinkled out of the dark sky as Lydia kept pace with Officer Jameson and his dog. A chill settled on her skin as her light spring jacket got wet. She didn't care if she was soaked to the bone, she wasn't leaving this forest until they found Elsie.

When she peered over her shoulder, three other dogs and their owners were headed in the same general direction they were going. One of the dog handlers wore a gun belt and a police uniform. The other two, dressed in street clothes, must be search and rescue volunteers. Officer Jameson had phoned one of the searchers and told them to stay behind and watch the parking lot. There had been two other cars besides the bus. That was smart. It could be that the kidnappers had parked on a turnout down the mountain road, but if whoever had taken Elsie had parked in that lot, they wouldn't be able to get to their vehicle without being spotted. It would be far easier to catch someone fleeing on foot. Officer Jameson seemed to think of everything.

His yellow Lab never lost concentration as they hurried through the trees on the other side of the meadow.

They headed down a grassy hill. Lydia's feet pounded the ground. Up ahead, she could see a shallow river.

When they arrived at the creek, the yellow Lab stopped.

The K-9 raised her nose in the air then sat down on her haunches.

"What's going on?"

"I'm not sure," said Officer Jameson. "I think she lost the scent."

"Because of the creek?" She tried to keep the rising panic out of her voice. Elsie was here. She had to be.

He shook his head. "A trained nose can follow a scent through water."

"The rain maybe?" She scrambled for an explanation.

"It just started. It can't be more than forty minutes since…since the incident. The scent would still be red hot."

Lydia felt like she was falling down a cliff all over again. "Then what?" She appreciated that Officer Jameson was sensitive enough not to use the word *abduction* when speaking about what had happened to Elsie. Still, her mind raced with images of what might have happened to her precious daughter, her world.

The other dogs arrived at the creek, demonstrating a similar reaction.

A lump formed in her throat.

I'm not leaving these woods without my daughter. She has to be here.

"I'm not sure." River stepped toward one of the other volunteer searchers, a stout, forty-something woman dressed in workout gear. Her German shepherd sat at attention beside her. "Did you bring the ball cap?"

"Lenny has it." She gestured toward an older muscular man with a border collie, another of the volunteers. The blond woman wearing a gun belt was with a golden retriever. She wore a dark green windbreaker with a tan logo that said COK9TF. Officer Jameson was wearing the same type of jacket.

River got the ball cap and placed it close to Frankie's nose. The dog put her nose to the ground and moved in a circle, but her tail never wagged.

The blond woman stepped up to Officer Jameson. "There's a road over there. Maybe—" The blond officer glanced at Lydia.

Something in Lydia's demeanor must have communicated that she was the distraught mother without introductions having to be made.

River shook his head. "The dogs would have picked up the scent and gone toward the road if there had been a car waiting there and Elsie was put in it."

The road did explain how someone could have gotten to the cliff without being spotted.

"We have to keep looking, Officer Jameson," said Lydia.

"Call me River. We're not giving up." He reached out and squeezed her forearm. The kindness she saw in his blue eyes was comforting. His voice had a calming effect on her. She needed to brush away any dark thoughts. Elsie was okay. They were going to find her.

The other dogs were exposed to the ball cap again. River directed Frankie toward the road. The K-9 lowered her nose to the ground, took a few steps and then looked up at River. It was clear she wasn't picking up on anything.

Lydia fought off the sense of despair she felt. River returned to her while the other handlers led their dogs around the area where the scent had gone cold. He didn't have to say anything for her to know what was going on. It appeared that her daughter had vanished into thin air.

Her phone dinged. She pulled it out. The text was from Angel.

She read the text. "It's from my co-teacher. They had to take the other kids back to the school before the parents showed up. She's going to come back up in her car to take me home." She rested her palm on her chest as her voice faltered. "She asked if Elsie had been found."

"I can take you home." River's voice flooded with compassion.

None of the dogs had picked up on anything. There must be something else they could do.

She turned to face River. "Has this ever happened before with the K-9s? Be honest with me."

"I'm not sure what's going on. Frankie's nose is second to none." He pointed at the blond woman with the golden retriever. "Officer Reynolds' K-9 is trained to track in all kinds of conditions. I'll see to it that choppers are called in to continue the search. We'll keep going through the night. Let me take you home first, though. I'd like to get some more information about Elsie that could help the search."

Her whole body tensed. The scent was gone. Would they just be running around in circles?

She nodded as numbness set in. She just couldn't process that her daughter had been abducted. Who would do such a thing? "I need to text Angel."

The phone screen blurred as she pressed the buttons.

No sign of Elsie. I have a ride home.

The answer came back a second later.

So sorry. Call me. I have something to tell you that might be important.

Hope glimmered for Lydia as she pressed Angel's number. River was standing close. "She has something to tell me that might help." She pressed the speaker button so River could hear, too.

Angel's voice came across the line. "Lydia. I'm so sorry this is happening."

Lydia cleared her throat. "Thank you. What is it you had to tell me?"

"Miles said when we sat down to have our lunch, he saw an old lady's head pop up from behind the bushes over by the trees."

Lydia could feel her hope deflating like a balloon losing air. Four-year-old Miles had a habit of making things up to draw attention to himself. She whispered to River. "Miles is one of my students."

River leaned toward the phone. "Officer Jameson here. Did the little boy give any more details?"

"He just said that the lady had white hair."

"Thank you, Angel."

"I'll keep praying, my friend," said Angel. "Don't you worry about your class. I'll take care of things. I'm sure the school will understand that you need time off."

"I appreciate that." Lydia pressed the disconnect button. Her voice gave away the level of despair that she felt.

"Something wrong?" River was still standing close to her.

She shrugged and shook her head. "It's just that Miles tends to tell stories so he can be in the spotlight."

River nodded. "Okay. It could be he made it up. It could be he did see someone, and she had nothing to do with what happened here today. We're just gathering information at this point." He squeezed her arm above the elbow. "I'm going to call my supervisor to see if I can take lead on this investigation since I was first on the scene."

Lydia nodded. That he wanted to be in charge suggested

that he felt a strong connection to Elsie's case. He stepped way to make the call and then returned to her.

"Let me give the others instructions and then I'll take you home." With Frankie heeling beside him, River gestured for the group to come toward him.

She was shivering by the time they headed back through the trees toward the trail. They stood at his patrol car. A news van had pulled into the parking lot. Being interviewed was the last thing she felt up to doing.

"I can handle them, if you want me to. It would be good to have Elsie's face on the news," said River.

"Thank you." She handed River her phone with Elsie's picture on it.

River spoke with the news crew and then returned to where Lydia waited.

"Why don't you take that wet coat off? I have a blanket for you."

She got into the front passenger side of the patrol car, holding the wet coat in her hands. River loaded Frankie into the kennel in back, reached for something on the floor of the back seat and then opened the driver's-side door.

He handed her a blanket still in the plastic wrap. She opened it up and placed it around her shoulders. Though River only wore a dark green windbreaker, he didn't appear to be affected by the rain. The windbreaker had a tan logo on the back that read COK9TF, the same as the woman River had called Lizzie. She wondered what it meant.

As they headed down the mountain, River radioed for more ground searchers and helicopters. He put the radio back into its slot. "I have some police business to take care of in town and then I'll go back and help with the search. Text me so I have your phone number."

She pulled out her phone, and he spoke his number.

A silence settled into the car. She could see the outskirts of Ridge up ahead.

River cleared his throat. "I have to ask. Is there anyone who would want to take your daughter?"

The question was like a spike being driven through her heart. "I have an ex-husband who wasn't happy about me getting full custody of Elsie. But he's in rehab right now."

"Still, something we need to check out," said River. "What's the name of the rehab?"

"Second Chances, in Boulder. His name is Sloane Caldwell."

"That boy said the woman was old with white hair. What about your ex's parents?"

"They weren't happy about me divorcing Sloane. They thought I should have hung in there. Sheryl's hair isn't white, though. It's strawberry-blond. Whatever their feelings are toward me, they dote on Elsie."

He nodded. "I'm just trying to think of every angle."

"It can't be them. I got a text from them yesterday saying they were headed to see their daughter in Grand Junction. She just had a baby." She massaged her temple.

"Do you have any other relatives who might have white hair or a reason to take Elsie?"

She shook her head. "I have no other family. It's just me and Elsie."

His features softened. Was that compassion or pity she saw in his face?

Lydia's mind raced. "Maybe it's not personal. Maybe someone was on that mountain looking for the chance to take any child, watching and waiting for one of the children to be away from the group." Even vocalizing the theory made her stomach tie in a knot.

"Like I said, all avenues have to be explored, but in these initial hours, our focus is on searching for your daughter."

River turned onto Main Street. And then took a side street.

"My house is just a couple of blocks up this street and then take a right, 407 Weston."

He rolled to a stop in front of her house. "I'll walk you to your door. Ridge police will have to get a statement from you at some point."

They stood on her front steps, facing each other. "My daughter is alive and we're going to find her." Her voice lacked conviction.

River nodded. "I'm concerned about your safety because you were pushed off that cliff. I'll make sure the local police run a patrol past your house."

"Do you really think someone will come after me again? I think they just needed to get me out of the way so they…so they—" Her throat went tight. "So they could get to Elsie."

The reality that her daughter had been kidnapped was beginning to sink in. She just couldn't fathom that her life was also in danger. The tears flowed and turned into body-shaking sobs.

River patted her arm and spoke softly. "The tears are understandable. This is a lot to carry."

Overwhelmed with emotion, she fell against his chest, and he wrapped his arms around her. Though her actions had been impulsive, she relished the safety she felt in River's arms. It had been a long time since she'd been held. Not that Sloane had shown her much affection even before the marriage exploded and she found herself alone.

She pulled back. Her cheeks grew hot when she looked into his eyes. "Sorry I just—" She smoothed her shirtfront, embarrassed that she had fallen into the arms of a man she barely knew. She stared at the ground.

"It's okay. Don't be embarrassed. You held it together pretty good the whole time we were searching." He turned to go. "I'll stay in touch with you."

She pulled her key from the pocket of her jeans. She hadn't taken her purse on the hike. Only her license and house key. She turned the knob to open the door. River was halfway down her sidewalk when he pivoted back to her. "Lock your doors. Just a precaution."

"Yes, of course." She didn't want to believe that her life was under threat.

She stepped inside the dark room. Reminders of Elsie were everywhere, from her favorite stuffed animal to the crayon pictures on the refrigerator. She fell face-first onto the sofa and prayed through the flowing tears.

Oh, God. Please bring my little girl back to me. She's all I have.

As he drove toward the burger place to do his interview with Danielle Potter, River could not get his mind off of Lydia. The comment about not having any family had stabbed at his heart. He'd do anything to end her agony and see light come back into those green eyes. He could still see the photograph of Elsie in his mind. Though he couldn't neglect his duties to the task force, his mind was on finding Elsie. He *had* to find her.

The Ridge police had given him permission to take lead on Elsie's case, but he'd have to run it by his task force supervisor too.

Only a few cars were parked in the lot of Ridge Burgers and More. Before he went inside, he pulled up the phone number for Second Chances rehab and called. He identified himself to the woman who answered and asked if Sloane Caldwell was at their facility.

A pert female voice responded, "What is this concerning?"

"An investigation involving a kidnapping of his daughter."

"Oh my. I can tell you that Mr. Caldwell has been here for over a week, and he's not allowed to leave the facility or make phone calls at this early stage of the program. He's had no news from the outside world as per the protocol of the program. The only reason we break that rule is for death in the family. Finding out about his daughter could lead to relapse."

"I understand. I just need to know if he had the opportunity to leave the facility."

"I can talk to staff and see if he was present at his meetings today."

"Thank you." He recited his number and hung up.

He drew his attention back to the nearly empty parking lot of Ridge Burgers and More. It was well past the lunch hour. After deploying Frankie, he pushed through the glass doors and stepped up to the counter. Only two tables were occupied. One with a mom and two kids, and the other with an older gentleman eating alone. The scent of salt and grease hung in the air.

A boy of about sixteen stood behind the cash register. "Welcome to Ridge Burgers. What can I get for you?"

River pulled his badge. "I'm looking for Danielle Potter."

"Oh yeah, she said a cop would be coming by. She's in the back, cleaning the fryer. I'll tell her you're here."

The boy disappeared and a moment later a woman with brown hair twisted into braids, arched eyebrows and a nose ring emerged. Her rich brown eyes had a sparkle to them. She couldn't have been more than twenty years old. "Officer Jameson?"

He nodded.

After filling a paper cup with soda, Danielle came around the counter and pointed at an empty table. "We can just sit here. I'm due to take my break anyway. I have fifteen minutes."

River took a seat and Frankie sat at attention beside him.

"Cute dog."

Frankie thumped her tail.

Having his partner close always seemed to break the ice with people. "You called the task force because you thought you learned something about Gayle that might be helpful."

She took a sip of her drink. "Gayle and I were friendly, but we weren't friends. You know what I mean?"

"So, you didn't get together outside work?"

"Exactly, but we got along real well, and she was always chatty when we worked a shift together. I've been thinking about it ever since I saw the news article about her body being found on that hiking trail."

"So why did you contact us now?" River was afraid this interview was going to be a dead end. He was losing valuable time when he could have been helping look for Elsie.

"Shortly before she quit, she showed me a picture of a guy she was with. Said his name was Joel. She was really falling hard for him. I think she was already pregnant by then, since she started bringing a healthy lunch to work instead of the fast food we serve here, which she could have had for free. I think Joel was the father."

"Joel?" A first name wasn't much to go on. The task force didn't have a lot of information on the murdered teens due to their strained relationships with families. "Do you remember the photograph? What did he look like?"

She moved her hand closer to his and leaned in. Frankie licked her chops and scooted closer, her attention on Danielle. "I don't have to remember the photograph because yesterday he came in here to pick up an online order. He was kind of jumpy. Maybe he was on drugs. Maybe he was nervous about being back in the place where his murdered girlfriend had worked."

Joel didn't sound like a very stable person. "Do you think he killed her?"

"He didn't seem like the type, kind of timid. I do remember that Gayle said she was concerned about his drug use. Drugs do change people's personalities, so maybe he could have found out about the baby after it was born and killed her when he was high." She shrugged. "I don't know. I liked Gayle. Maybe we could've been friends if she'd lived. I want to help."

"Tell me what he looked like."

"Short brown hair, acne. Kind of tall and skinny. Oh, and I have this." She dug through the pockets of her apron and handed him what looked like a receipt. "He ordered from an online app where you have to give your full name."

River stared at the receipt. Joel Henley. He had a first and last name. Danielle had saved the most important detail for last. "Thank you. This will help us."

Danielle smiled and took another sip of her drink. "It would be good to get justice for Gayle and maybe find out what happened to her baby."

Frankie released a whimper that sounded like a vote of agreement.

"We all want that for Gayle and the other young women who were taken too soon," said River.

He thanked her, bringing the interview to a close, then headed out the door with Frankie heeling beside him. Once inside his patrol car, he phoned his task force boss with the information Danielle had given him.

Emmett Dane's voice came across the line. "We'll get Eva on this right away to see if she can track down an address for Joel Henley." In addition to being the head of the task force, Emmett was an FBI agent based out of Denver. Eva Gomez was the task force's tech specialist.

"Sounds good," said River. "Even if Joel is trying not to be found, Eva will be able to track him down."

"Once we have a solid address for him, I want you to partner with Maren. Her K-9 might be required if things get ugly."

Maren Anderson, whom he'd only met recently when they'd both joined the task force, was a good cop. Her K-9 Haven, a Doberman pinscher, was trained in both narcotics and suspect apprehension. "I'd be glad to have them along." He took in a breath. "Did you hear about the abduction case here in Ridge?"

"Yes, Lizzie called me."

"I asked the Ridge police if I could take lead on this case."

"A three-year-old girl is involved. I think it would be good for you to work this case." Emmett knew what had happened with Noah. Maybe that was why he'd said yes.

"I know it will take time away from the task force case."

"We'll manage. We'll try to provide as much support as we can to get it wrapped up quickly. If Eva has the time, she can help you track down information."

"Thank you, Emmett."

River disconnected and checked his texts. He had two of them. The first was from Second Chances.

Sloane made all his meetings and showed up for his check-ins.

That ruled out the husband. It would have to be someone who'd known about the field trip. Someone at the school? Another parent? The other possibility was that it was a crime of opportunity by a stranger who made a habit of taking children.

The thought gave him chills.

The second text was a single word from Lydia.

Anything?

River's breath hitched as if a vise was being tightened around his chest. The photograph of Noah was burned into his memory as well. He covered his eyes with his hand.

Oh, God, I don't want to repeat history. Help me find this little girl.

He phoned his colleague Lizzie, hoping for something positive he could text to Lydia. If the child had been located, he would have been informed right away. But maybe they'd found a shoe or a coat, anything that might give Lydia hope.

"Any news?" River managed to speak in a strong voice despite the doubt and fear he wrestled with.

"We questioned the owners of the other two cars in the lot. They were high up on the trail and didn't see anything. A farmer did notice a car coming out where that dirt road meets up with the pavement about the time of the abduction."

If that car was connected to the kidnapping, Elsie could be miles from Ridge by now…or worse. "What kind of car?"

"The farmer was too far away to see details. He just said it was dark-colored."

"Frankie and I are coming back up there. I want to take another run at figuring out why she lost the scent."

"We got two more volunteer teams, additional officers and two choppers. We'll keep up the search for now, but if that car had anything to do with the kidnapping, the kid's not here anymore."

That reality caused his stomach to knot. "I get what

you're saying. We need to shift strategies and for that we need more information. My skills might be better utilized figuring out why the girl was taken."

"The mother would be a good place to start," said Lizzie.

"I've questioned her a little." It was the reason he'd offered to drive her home. "She could provide leads for who at the school might be involved. If this abduction wasn't random, it had to be someone who knew about the field trip."

"The plan is to keep up the search until it gets too dark to see. It would be good if we had options before we call off the search for the night. I'll let you know if anything shifts."

"Thanks. I'll keep you in the loop as well," said River.

River disconnected and stared at his phone. Any message he gave Lydia, he wanted to deliver in person.

Right now, he had nothing but bad news for her.

THREE

Lydia had somehow fallen asleep—likely due to stress—on the couch when the doorbell rang. She bolted up and hurried across the wooden floor. Through the window by the door, she saw River standing with Frankie by his side.

She touched her face. Her eyes were puffy from crying.

River held a pizza box in his hands. "Thought you might be hungry."

The aroma of Italian spices and pepperoni floated through the air. She hadn't eaten since the morning. "It is past dinnertime, isn't it?" She stepped aside so he and Frankie could enter. How had so much time passed so quickly?

After closing the door, she hurried into the kitchen. "I'll get us something to drink."

"The pizza might be a little cold. Parking is at a premium in this neighborhood. I had to park my patrol car three blocks away."

She stared out the window at the gray sky. "Everyone's getting home from work." She pulled some tea out of the fridge. "I assume this isn't just about bringing me dinner. You probably have more questions for me. Have the searchers learned anything new?" He hadn't answered her text, which made her fear that he wanted to deliver bad news in person.

He set the pizza box on the table and stepped closer to her, his expression grim.

"It's starting to look like Elsie was taken away in a car on that road."

Lydia gripped the corner of the counter. River rushed to her side and took the pitcher of tea. He touched her back lightly to steady her. He set the tea by the pizza on the table.

Frankie rushed toward Lydia and stared up at her with rich brown eyes. She offered her a tail wag. Lydia reached down and stroked the yellow Lab's head. "Aren't you sweet."

"She's pretty good at picking up on the emotions in a room." He pulled a chair out and flipped open the pizza box. "Why don't you sit down?"

Feeling numb, she managed a nod and moved toward the table. River found some glasses and plates and sat kitty-corner from her.

Even though the scent of the pizza was enticing, and she hadn't had any food for hours, the thought of eating didn't appeal to her.

River placed a slice of pizza on her plate and poured the drinks. She took a couple of small bites. "I'll do anything to find my daughter. What do you need to know?"

"Since we've ruled out relatives, I need a rundown on anyone who might have known about the field trip. Parents and other teachers, neighbors."

She didn't have to ask to know that each name would be checked out for criminal history, including child abduction or abuse or…worse.

She stared down at her pizza and then looked into River's blue eyes, shaking her head. "What if she's cold? What if she's hungry?"

"Don't let your mind go there. You'll shut down. Let's

focus on what we can do. Think of anyone who might have something against you."

Lydia nodded. She ate a little more pizza while she wracked her brain. "At the beginning of the school year, there was a kid who drowned in a pond while we were on a field trip. The death was due to a seizure. There was nothing anyone could have done, but Tyler's father blamed the school and me in particular. He was kind of a hothead anyway. I was the lead teacher for that trip."

"What's the guy's name?"

"Prentiss Grafton. Tyler's mom was not in the picture. I was at a school event, and Prentiss came on to me. This was before the accident with his son. I'm not interested in dating anyone. He seemed pretty upset when I spurned his advances. That might be why I became a target after his son's death."

River wrote down the name. "We'll check him out."

"The field trip was posted on the class schedule. Anyone who walked through the school and peered into my classroom might have seen it."

"That makes the suspect list pretty long," said River. He wrote down the names of the other teachers and staff that she gave him, but she doubted any of them were involved.

He seemed capable…she could only pray he'd find Elsie. Again, she wondered which agency he was with.

She pointed to the COK9TF badge on his windbreaker. "So, what's this about? I thought you worked for the Ridge police force. That other searcher, the blond lady, had a jacket just like it."

"I do work for the local PD, but this is for a task force put together with officers throughout Colorado. I'm sure you've seen the stories of the teenaged girls who were killed shortly after they gave birth."

"Yes. I remember when Gayle Gorman's body was found outside of Ridge."

"There were two other girls. Jenny Clarke from Canyon Creek and Nina Olson from Colorado Springs. And now we have a missing girl from Denver who we think is still alive, Mia Andrews." River got a faraway look in his eyes.

Elsie wasn't the only missing person he was dealing with. She prayed they found the missing teen as well.

When she looked out the window, the sky had grown dark. They'd talked for a long time. Lydia tensed after glancing at the kitchen clock. Every hour that passed meant the chances of finding her girl got slimmer. She had to cling to hope. She had to.

"What is your experience with this? You've found children alive even after a day has passed, haven't you?"

"Every case is different." He looked away and then stared at the floor. There was something he was keeping from her.

And sometimes the outcome isn't good, she thought.

She rose to her feet, crossed the kitchen and stared out the window at her backyard. She'd totally forgotten to turn on the water for her fledgling raspberries, something she always did when she got home from work. Maybe doing the routine caretaking of her yard would quell the fear that ambushed her over and over.

"I'll be right back. I just got to turn hoses on. My raspberries are hanging on by a thread." As was she. Lydia hurried out the back door and down the walkway to turn the spigot. The spring air and nighttime quiet was like a soothing balm to her.

Lydia raised her head when she thought she sensed movement nearby. Suddenly someone grabbed her and pulled her backward. A gloved hand went over her mouth so she couldn't cry out. She reached for the garden bench, grabbing a trowel.

Inside the house, she heard Frankie bark.

Lydia twisted her body and used the trowel to hit the assailant's arm. He held on and dragged her backward toward the trees that bordered her house. The man grasped her in an iron grip. Her heart pounded. The sky seemed to whirl around her.

She heard the dog barking. Frankie was getting closer. The man let go of her and pushed her to the ground. She fell onto her stomach.

River ran past her, Frankie on his heels. "You all right?"

She managed a faint, "Yes."

He shouted a command at Frankie, who stopped close to her and licked her face. She reached out to the yellow Lab. "You're going to be my protector."

She pushed herself to her feet and ran back to the house with Frankie by her side, where she intended to call the police.

When she glanced over her shoulder, River had disappeared into the trees where the attacker had gone. She only hoped he was able to catch him and not be hurt himself. It would take at least ten minutes for the police to arrive.

This had to be connected to Elsie's abduction. One thing was clear now. She was a target, too. Someone wanted her dead.

The darkness in the forest was disorienting to River as he scanned the spaces between the trees and waited for his eyes to adjust to the lack of light. The person who had attacked Lydia seemed to have disappeared. He pulled his gun and listened for the sound of footfalls. He could have used Frankie's keen senses, but he'd feared the attacker might double back and take another shot at Lydia. Frankie wasn't trained in protection, but there was nothing like a barking dog to deter a criminal.

He turned his head, still not hearing anything. The forest must be fairly deep. He couldn't see where it ended. If the attacker was running away, he would have heard it.

Still on high alert, he stepped deeper into the trees, turning his head and tuning his ears to any change around him. A bird fluttered out of a branch above him. His heart pounded when he looked up.

A weight crashed against him, knocking him to the ground on his back. The gun had slipped from his hand. The man was on top of him. With one hand, River patted the ground, hoping to find his weapon. With his free hand, he braced it beneath the man's chin, curving his neck backward and keeping him from getting closer to River's face.

The attacker swiped at River's arm, causing him to lose his grip. He brought the other hand up before the man could reach for his throat. The assailant landed a single blow to River's jaw, triggering pain that vibrated through his head.

River sought to twist his body in an effort to get out from underneath the other man while he swung a closed fist at his attacker's face. The blow landed on the man's nose. The attacker lifted his weight. River flipped over to his stomach. He saw the glint of metal in the moonlight. His gun. He crawled toward it.

The attacker grabbed him by his collar, choking him with his shirt. River wheezed. His hand was only inches from his gun when the attacker landed a blow to his head with a hard object. White dots filled his field of vision. He could feel himself fading as the man hit him again with the object. This time on his back and shoulders.

Then he heard the sound of a barking dog. Frankie.

He reached for his gun. It felt heavy in his hand. He did not want to lose consciousness.

Sirens wailed, growing louder and closer. A heavy object fell by his head; the log that had been used as a weapon. He heard the sound of retreating footsteps. He turned in time to see the man dressed in dark clothing disappear into the trees.

Frankie reached him and licked his face.

"Are you okay?" Lydia's voice was sweeter than honey as she knelt and extended a hand toward him.

He groaned. "You could have been hurt."

"Frankie and I got worried. After I called the police, I realized I couldn't leave you out here alone. I know these woods." She helped him to his feet.

Pain shot through his head and back. With Lydia supporting him and Frankie heeling beside him, whimpering and casting concerned glances up at him, River made it back to the house, where he gave the waiting police officers a quick rundown of what had happened. Both patrol cars took off to try to catch the fleeing man.

Lydia retrieved an ice pack for River to press against the knot on his head, then she handed him a glass of water and some pain pills. "Do you think you should go to the ER to be checked out?"

"I'll be fine. Did you get a look at the guy?"

"Not a good look. The hoodie covered his face, and it was dark. He was tall and he was strong."

"That would be my assessment, too. Definitely a male, and probably a younger guy." He winced.

"Prentiss Grafton is my age and in good shape." She couldn't believe the man would do something this horrible.

River winced again.

From where she sat facing him on the sofa, she reached

out to touch his forearm, her face filled with concern. "Are you sure you don't want to go to the doctor?"

Her touch warmed his skin. "I'm sure. I'll be all right." The truth was he didn't want to leave her alone as long as the attacker was still out there.

Lydia's forehead wrinkled, and she laced her fingers together. "This must be related to what happened to Elsie. I guess it's pretty clear that I'm a target, too. Whoever pushed me over that cliff intended to kill me. When he didn't succeed, he took a second shot at me."

"He must not have known I was here. I had to park the patrol car so far from the house."

She bent forward and rested her face in her hands. "Who would do this?"

He asked her about other aspects of her life. The church she attended, the gym she worked out at. His thoughts returned again to Lydia's angry ex-husband. "Do you think he might have sent someone to take Elsie?"

She nodded. "Yes, maybe. Sloane is an angry man who never takes responsibility for his actions. Right before he went into rehab, he was served the papers that said I got sole custody. He knew it was going to happen, but getting the papers probably made it more real and could have pushed him over the edge."

He'd have to call Second Chances again to see if any of the other patients had gone AWOL.

His phone rang. One of the Ridge officers. The attacker had not been found. He ended the call. "I think it's best I stay here with you tonight."

She rose to her feet. "I'll get you a pillow and a blanket."

After handing River the bedding, Lydia retreated to her bedroom.

He walked the perimeter of the house with Frankie,

searching the trees that connected with her backyard. He stared at the dark forest for a long moment. Would the attacker come back again tonight? He retrieved some of Frankie's food from the patrol car.

Once inside, he watched the street through Lydia's front window while Frankie ate her meal. Satisfied that he didn't see anything suspicious, he settled down on the sofa, placing his gun on the side table for easy access. Frankie lay on the floor beside the sofa.

If anyone tried to break in again, the Lab would sound the alarm. Even if Lydia was safe tonight, the one thing River was sure of was that the man who had tried to kill her twice would return.

FOUR

Lydia awoke to the sound of her phone ringing. She reached for it on her nightstand. Her first thought was that Elsie had been found.

She sat up in bed. Frankie sat at attention watching her. The dog must have wandered in through the open door.

She looked at the number. Her mother-in-law, Sheryl.

"Hello."

"Oh, my heart, Lydia. We just saw on the news."

In the chaos that followed Elsie's disappearance, she had not thought to call the grandparents.

"I'm sorry. I should have phoned you," said Lydia. Despite there being tension over Lydia divorcing their son, Norm and Sheryl were good grandparents and the only family support that Lydia had.

"No, I'm sure you had enough on your mind. Dear sweet Elsie. Both Norm and I are just beside ourselves. How could this happen?" Sheryl's voice cracked.

How indeed. Sheryl Caldwell's agitation did not have a calming effect on Lydia. The older woman was prone to over-the-top reactions anyway. "I don't know." Lydia felt the all too familiar tightening in her chest.

"You poor thing. Is anyone there with you, a friend perhaps?"

"There's a police officer here with me, but I'm sure he needs to get back to work."

"So, you'll be alone. That's what I thought. We've already left Grand Junction and are on our way over to be with you."

"Oh, Sheryl. I appreciate that so much, but I'm sure Debbie could use the help as well." Sloane's sister had had a preemie baby recently who required lots of extra care. Lydia knew the couple had been staying with her.

"Nonsense. We're on our way. We can go back to see Debbie another time."

The gesture touched Lydia greatly. Most of her interaction with Norm and Sheryl was because of Elsie. Now they seemed concerned about her. Maybe they were letting go of their anger over her divorcing their son. "Thank you, Sheryl. I appreciate that."

"You need family around at a time like this." Sheryl let out a wavering breath, and her voice trembled as she added, "Who would do such a thing to that precious little girl?"

Sheryl's heightened emotional response was stirring Lydia up. She closed her eyes and gripped the phone, barely able to get the words out. "I wish I knew."

"We'll get there as fast as we can. You take care of yourself."

"Thank you, Sheryl. I appreciate you and Norm so much. I'll call you if there's any news on Elsie. I'm so sorry I didn't keep you in the loop in the first place."

They said their goodbyes and Lydia hit the disconnect button. Lydia looked down at Frankie, who had been watching her intently. "Did you come in to check on me?" She knelt and stroked Frankie's ears. "What a good girl."

Lydia walked into her bathroom to wash her face.

The scent of bacon and coffee filled the air when she stepped into the kitchen, where River stood at the stove.

"Hope you don't mind. I thought you could use some breakfast."

"Not at all. It's nice to have someone cook a meal for me." Even on the days that he'd gotten up in time for work, Sloane had usually been so hung over that she ate breakfast alone. There had never been a time when he'd cooked for her. She'd never felt so lonely as when she'd been married to Sloane.

River turned to the coffeepot after grabbing a mug from a cupboard. "What do you take in your liquid energy?"

She studied him for a moment. The firm jaw and look of concentration indicated a highly focused man who was good at his job. But the tousled blond hair, which looked like he'd combed it with his fingers, suggested a relaxed side to his personality. There was something endearing about a man who didn't fuss about his appearance. The total effect made him attractive.

She felt a check in her spirit. River's kindness drew her in, but after what she'd been through with Sloane, she'd vowed not to give her heart to a man ever again. She'd had enough pain for a lifetime.

She combed her fingers through her red hair involuntarily. Okay. So, she was conscious of how she looked when she was around the handsome officer but that didn't mean she had to do anything about it.

"Black is fine." She intended to drink her coffee slowly, hoping it would help her get beyond the anxiety over her daughter still missing. She had no intention of going to work today. Angel had said she'd take care of everything at the school. All the same, she probably should at least check in with Angel at some point. Right now, her job was the last thing on her mind.

River handed her the cup of coffee. "Take a seat. I have

things under control. Your kitchen is organized very logically, just like you would expect of someone who works with preschoolers."

His compliment brought a smile to her face. She sat down. A second later, River placed a plate in front of her that had bacon, toast and eggs on it. He sat down across from her with his own plate.

"Can we say grace?"

"Sure. That would be great," he said.

She'd suspected that he was a man of faith. Now she knew for sure. Lydia bowed her head.

"Lord, we thank You for this food. Please be with the police and the people looking for Elsie." A lump formed in her throat. "Bring my little girl home."

River placed his hand over hers. The warmth of his touch calmed her.

He took a few bites of food and offered Frankie a tiny nibble of bacon. "I need to deal with some task force business today. I got a call from our tech. She's tracked down the address for Gayle Gorman's boyfriend."

She took a sip of her coffee enjoying the robust flavor. "So sad about Gayle." Of course, he had to get back to work. Having River and Frankie close had been such a comfort to her. She'd been able to sleep deeply knowing he was watching out for her.

"My in-laws are going to try to get over here soon. I might call a friend to be with me today as well."

"I already called the Ridge police department. They'll be able to spare an officer to sit outside in a patrol car." He checked his watch. "She should be here shortly."

"Thank you for setting that up."

"As soon as I deal with this task force interview, all my attention will be on following the different leads we came up with last night. As a favor to me, Eva, the tech analyst on the COK9 task force, is doing a background and alibi check on Prentiss Grafton."

River seemed to be putting a great deal of energy into finding Elsie, almost above and beyond what was expected of him professionally. As if the case were deeply personal to him. "It must be rewarding when you find a lost child."

"Yes, sure. When that happens, it's a cause for joy." He glanced off to the side and bent his head.

Her question seemed to cause a mood shift. "But that's not always the case, right?" Even asking the question opened the door to the possibility that Elsie might not be found.

His voice dropped half an octave. "No, sometimes there are not happy endings." He glanced at Frankie, who moved closer to him and licked his hand. A confirmation of some shared experience between partners who understood each other in a deep way.

"Oh?" She took a few bites of food, hoping he would say more. Silence fell between them for several minutes.

They finished their meal, exchanging small talk. She gathered up the dishes.

River waited for the Ridge officer to be in place. He stood with the door slightly ajar. "Lock this after I leave."

"Sure." She took several steps toward him.

"I'll be back in touch as soon as I can."

He stepped outside. After locking the door, she stood watching as River and Frankie walked up the street to where his patrol car was parked.

Clearly, he was a man with depth and perhaps a few secrets. Her gaze came to rest on the other patrol car parked on the street. She could see the female officer inside.

Hopefully, the police presence would be enough to deter another attempt on her life.

* * *

After putting Frankie in her kennel and entering Joel Henley's address in his GPS, River drove across town. Officer Maren Anderson with her narcotics K-9 had agreed to meet him at the address. As he got closer, the houses started to look a little more run-down, the lawns less pristine.

Maren was waiting in her patrol car when he pulled into the lot of the apartment building. When she spotted River, she got out of her car and deployed Haven, the reddish Doberman. Maren offered River a bright smile as she walked toward him. Her sweet demeanor and features often made people underestimate her as a police officer. With her long, honey-brown hair and blue eyes, she looked more like she should be teaching a class with Lydia rather than serving as the top-notch officer that she was. Her dimples only added to the effect. But River knew there was more to her than how she appeared. Recently, Maren's twin sister, a known addict, was assumed to have died. She was believed to have drowned in a river, which was the last place she'd been seen.

River glanced around the lot and spotted the model car that Eva had tracked down as belonging to Joel. "Looks like he's here." He glanced at Maren. "How are you doing?" It couldn't be easy dealing with a case that might involve drugs two months after Opal's death.

Maren blinked and bit her lower lip. "I have a job to do. I know me and my sister weren't on the best terms, but I miss her."

He patted her arm. "I'm here if you need to talk. You know that."

The task force was barely a month old, but the twelve officers were already close even though they were spread across the state.

"Thank you, I appreciate that." Maren's attention went

back to the three-story building. "Let's approach with caution. He's on the third floor, so I doubt he'll try to jump."

River nodded. "I'll hang back in the hallway in case he gets past you."

Highly unlikely considering that Haven was cross-trained in suspect apprehension.

They entered the building and took the stairs at a brisk pace with Maren in the lead.

Once they found Joel's apartment, River stood out of sight down the hallway.

After drawing her weapon, Maren knocked on the door. "Joel Henley. Police. Open up."

Both dogs stood at attention, their gazes fixed on their partners, waiting for a command. River pulled his gun as well. Any time drugs were part of the scenario, things could escalate quickly.

A long moment passed.

Maren repeated her command. "Police. Open up."

The door swung open. River stepped forward, Frankie by his side.

"Whoa. Your dog is scary looking. I don't have anything on me. I've been clean for two weeks."

River moved in a few steps closer so Joel would see him. Joel had his hands in the air. Fear crossed Joel's features as he focused on Haven.

Maren shifted her weight. "Mind if my K-9 verifies that?"

The move was a smart one on Maren's part. If they did find drugs, it would give them leverage in questioning Joel. The potential of being charged with possession usually brought out the honesty in people.

Joel tugged on his ragged T-shirt and moved aside. Maren gave the command to Haven to search, and the dog went to work, skirting through the tiny apartment. Joel gave River a nervous glance when he stepped toward the open door with Frankie standing at attention by his side. He'd holstered his gun but left the strap open. Danielle had said that Joel seemed timid. That was the same impression River got.

Haven disappeared into a room that must be the bathroom. Kitchen, living room and bedroom were all in one cluttered open space.

Joel moved a pile of clothes to one side and slumped down on a worn love seat. "What is this all about anyway?"

"We have some questions for you about your former girlfriend, Gayle Gorman."

Joel rose from the love seat and paced toward the kitchen. "Look, I'm sorry about what happened to her, but she wasn't even really my girlfriend. She just got it into her head that we were a thing."

"But the baby she was pregnant with was your child?"

"Yes, I told her I wasn't ready to be a father. Like I said, we weren't actually dating. I was using a lot of drugs back then. I made stupid choices."

Maren and Haven emerged from the other room. "It's clean."

Joel picked up a dirty dish on the counter and placed it in the sink. "I feel bad for what happened to Gayle. I shouldn't have led her on." He turned to face the two officers. "I'm trying to be a more honorable guy from now on."

Something in Joel's tone of voice rang true to River. He was eaten up by guilt, trying to better himself. Still, even if he wasn't the killer, he might know something crucial about Gayle. "What did you think happened to Gayle when she disappeared?"

He shrugged. "She always talked about moving to California. When she stopped coming around, I just assumed that she'd taken off."

Maren stepped forward. A flash of fear came into Joel's eyes when Haven advanced beside her handler. River knew the K-9 was a sweetheart, but the stature and appearance of the red Doberman made her look threatening. "Did Gayle ever mention anyone following her or offering to help with pregnancy expenses?"

Joel thought for a moment then shook his head. "Not that I remember."

"What about free or sliding-scale clinics. Do you know if she was going anywhere for medical care?"

"Yeah, actually the last time I talked to her, she said there was a free clinic down in Denver that she really liked."

"She didn't happen to mention the name of it?"

Joel shook his head. "Just that it was in Denver and she had to take three buses to get there."

Not a strong lead but a lead all the same. The team had already started visiting free clinics in the region to ask if the victims had been patients and also to warn staff to be on the lookout for anyone offering help to young pregnant women. There was a lot of territory for the task force to cover but hopefully someone would remember Gayle.

River pulled out his business card. "Joel, thank you. If you remember anything else, even if you don't think it's important, give me or Officer Anderson a call."

Maren pulled out her business card as well.

Once they were outside, Maren said, "I know Joel seems like a guy trying to turn over a new leaf, but his whole attitude about the relationship and pregnancy breaks my heart. Gayle must have felt so alone."

"I know. I can picture her sitting on those buses going to all that trouble to get her baby medical care," said River. "We have to get justice for Gayle and Jenny and Nina and find Mia before it's too late. Those brave girls deserve that."

His throat grew tight. So many lives hung in the balance. He didn't want to revisit the anguish of losing another young person.

"Agreed. There's still a chance we can find Mia alive, but we have to work fast. I'll let Emmett know about checking out more free Denver clinics so he can get some team members on it. You probably want to get back to finding out to what happened to that other missing girl."

He nodded. "I know this is a time drain from the task force, but this is another young life that hangs in the balance. I have to find Elsie so she can be with her mother."

Noah's death had made him feel like he wasn't worthy of a family of his own, but maybe he could reunite other families.

Maren patted his arm. "All these lives matter."

"Thanks." He leaned a little closer to her. "Your sister's life mattered too. I know it's hard to work in the middle of grieving such a loss, but you and Haven did a good job in there today."

"Thank you," said Maren.

He gave her a quick hug and they parted ways.

He drove across town, intending to go back up to the search site to try one more time to see if Frankie's nose could tell him what had happened to Elsie. But first he needed to stop by Lydia's place and get something of Elsie's for Frankie to scent from.

As he pulled up to Lydia's house, he was glad to see the patrol car parked outside. When he knocked on the door, he was surprised when an older man with gray buzz cut answered the door.

Lydia came from the kitchen. "River, this is my father-in-law, Norm."

The man held his hand out to River, offering him a firm

handshake. "I came to give Lydia some support. My wife would have come, but she's pretty broken up about what's happened. I dropped her off at home so she could take a sedative."

Lydia stepped toward him. "Why did you come by? Is there news about Elsie?"

The look of hopeful expectation on Lydia's face sliced right through River. He shook his head. "The local PD are following up on some of the leads you gave us, and Eva is checking the histories of people connected to the school."

Norm touched Lydia's back. "I'm sure the police are doing everything they can."

"I'm heading back up where Elsie was last seen. I need something with her scent on it."

"I can get you that, but if you're going back up there, I'm going with you." Lydia strode over to where her jacket was hanging. She grabbed another smaller pink coat.

Arguing with the distraught mom would be pointless. Lydia needed to feel like she was doing something to find her daughter. She'd be safe with him.

She slipped into her jacket and handed River the pink coat. "Norm, you'll be all right?"

"Do what you have to do. I need to get back to check on Sheryl anyway. I'll lock up your place."

"Thank you," said Lydia.

Within twenty minutes, River and Lydia were headed back up the mountain road. He only hoped this time Frankie could get a clearer read on where Elsie had gone.

FIVE

Lydia ran to keep up with Frankie and River as they headed into the trees and back down to the creek. The yellow Lab had gone right to work despite Elsie's scent on the ground being twenty-four hours old.

Once again, the dog stopped at the creek. Despair encroached on Lydia's mind. Why had she hoped there would be a different result today?

They both stared out at the road where that car had probably been parked. "Officers are trying to see if anyone else might have seen that car up close," River said. "If we had a make and model, that would be helpful."

"I know you're doing everything you can." The numbness and the sensation that her brain was filled with cotton balls started all over again.

River stared across the creek. "There has to be something we haven't considered. An angle we haven't explored." He stepped across the creek and spoke to Frankie. "Find."

Frankie put her nose to the ground. At first, she moved in circles and paced back and forth, but then she trotted in a straight line, seemingly picking up on something. Lydia followed as they moved, coming to a tree with a posted No Trespassing sign. River commanded Frankie to stop.

Lydia came to stand beside River, close enough that their shoulders were touching. "What happened?"

"This is private land. We need to get permission from the owner to go on it."

When she looked over her shoulder, she saw that they had gone past a cluster of trees that would have hidden the sign from view from where they had stood at the creek yesterday.

She turned and stared out at the gently sloping land covered in brush and rocks. "Did she indicate she smelled anything?"

"She never alerted but she seemed to pick up on something. Maybe who ever owns this land was around yesterday and could help us."

It felt like River was grasping at straws. There were no visible structures on the property. The probability that someone had not only been out here but had seen something important seemed slim. "I suppose it would be easy enough to find out who owns the land." If straws were all they had, that is what they would reach for.

They headed back across the river and up the hill. An explosive noise penetrated the air. Frankie let out a bark as River tugged Lydia to the ground.

"We're being shot at." He pulled his gun. "Get over to those trees."

Her heart pounded as she pulled herself on her stomach with Frankie alongside her. When she peered over her shoulder, she saw that River was a few feet behind her. He'd drawn his gun and stopping every couple of seconds to peer around, probably trying to figure out where the shot had come from.

Another rifle shot made her crawl even faster. She rushed behind the cluster of trees. Frankie nestled close to her and licked her face. Having the dog by her side made her feel safer. When she looked out from behind a thick trunk, River half rose and fired off a shot. She glanced in the direction he'd fired, catching just a flash of movement by some rocks.

River ran the remaining distance and slipped in beside her. "We need to get back to the car and get out of here. Whoever is out there has a rifle. His range is way greater than my pistol."

He turned his head in the other direction, staring at the incline where there were a few bushes and rock piles. He touched her back. "Stay low. Move from one covered spot to another. Frankie will go with you. I'll be right behind you."

He locked her in his gaze. The iron resolve she saw there gave her courage. He kissed her forehead and touched her cheek lightly, locking her in his blue-eyed gaze. "Go. Be safe."

The kiss had been unexpected. She hurried up the hillside, dropping first behind some rocks and then a cluster of bushes. Another rifle shot filled the air. She could see a figure down below just before he or she slipped behind the cluster of trees they'd just been in. River had flattened himself against the ground.

Only the wind and the sound of her own intense breathing filled the air around her. After a long moment, River crawled up the mountain to her. Once behind the bushes, the land flattened out. They would have to make a run for it.

He nodded and she nodded back to show she understood what they needed to do. Frankie whimpered. They cautiously rose and sprinted across the meadow toward the trees that would lead to the trail connected with the parking lot.

Two more shots were fired in their direction. One came so close to Lydia that her eardrum hurt. She stepped to the side, not realizing how close she was to the steep drop-off. Her foot slipped. River reached for her, wrapping his arm around her waist and pulling her from the edge. Rocks tumbled down the cliff, crashing into each other.

Another shot echoed around them as they headed for the trees. They exited the trail and ran toward the parking lot.

River swung the back door open so Frankie could get in her kennel while Lydia ran around to the passenger side of the patrol car. He started the engine and pulled the radio, explaining the situation. "If we can get an officer out by that dirt road, maybe we can catch this guy."

The dispatcher's voice came out strong and clear. "We'll send an officer over there as quickly as possible."

He put the radio back in the slot and pressed the gas. "Let's get you out of harm's way."

The shooter had aimed for both her and River, which meant maybe they wanted River out of the way so they could get to her. When she glanced up the hill, she saw two hikers right before they disappeared over the hill. That explained the car that had arrived while they'd been on the other side of the trees. "Someone must have followed us from my house. How else would they have known where we were?"

River kept his eyes on the curving road up ahead. "I didn't see a car on that dirt road by the creek, though. Where did they park?"

River drove down the mountain then turned onto a road that was bordered by trees on both sides. In her peripheral vision, she saw a car on a dirt road that intersected with the road they were on. The tan vehicle blended into the trees and barely registered in her mind right before it zoomed forward and slammed into River's side of the patrol car.

Lydia screamed and gripped the armrest. Frankie let out a yelp of distress. The collision sent her side of the cruiser off the road, the incline leaving the patrol car at a precarious slant.

Her heart pounded when she peered through River's window as the older model, tan-colored SUV loomed toward them, preparing to knock them totally off the road.

River pressed the gas, hoping to avoid a second collision. The other vehicle impacted his back end, sending them down the incline and careening toward a tree. He braked, stopping short of hitting the tree.

Lydia glanced through the back window. Her face had gone white with fear. "He's coming toward us."

River looked up toward the road. The driver had gotten out of his SUV and was holding a rifle. He wore a ski mask, so his face wasn't visible. River pressed the button that would automatically open Frankie's kennel.

The man raised the rifle.

"Out your side," he said. The patrol car would provide a degree of cover.

The first bullet pierced the window, shattering it. Lydia was already on the ground. She opened the back door so Frankie could jump out. River crawled out her side of the car, dropped to the ground and pulled his gun as the side window in the back seat shattered. If Lydia hadn't acted so fast, Frankie would have been dead.

River lifted his head to peer through to windows to get a bead on where the shooter was. The man's SUV was parked perpendicular to his on the wrong side of the road. He scanned all around. Where had the shooter gone?

The breaking of a branch alerted him. The man had come down into the trees and was taking aim at them.

They sprinted around to the back bumper with Frankie following. Both of them were out of breath from the threat of death. He tilted his head around the cruiser to try to locate the shooter.

A shot came so close that his face burned.

A long, tense silence enveloped them. They were at a point of standoff. The rifle had enough range that the shooter did not have to move in closer. He just had to wait until they tried to make a run for it. "We can wait him out," River whispered.

"What if he decides to arc around into the forest so he can get a shot at us back here?" Lydia pointed to the trees as her voice laced with fear.

Would the man be so bold as to do that? To stay out of range of River's handgun, he'd have to go deep into the trees. He studied the area in front of him for a long moment. The sound of pounding footsteps caused him to drag his attention back up to the road. The shooter was running back to his SUV.

"Stay here." River hurried up the steep dirt incline in time to see the man get in his vehicle and pull away. River aimed his gun and took a shot. When he peered up the road, he saw the reason the attacker had sought escape. A Ridge police car was coming out of the same intersecting dirt road the shooter had emerged from. That must be the backup he'd called for. The officer had traveled the whole length of the dirt road.

River waved him down. The officer opened his window, his engine still running.

"Tan SUV. Maybe you can catch him."

The officer nodded, pulling forward and switching on his sirens. River hurried back down to Lydia. She fell into his arms. Her whole body was shaking.

"That was scary."

"I know." He held her until the trembling stopped.

She pulled away and looked into his eyes. Kissing her on the forehead had been impulsive. He'd wanted her to know he had her back, that he would keep her safe. He pressed his hand against her cheek.

"Let's get you home. I think we can maneuver this car back onto the road."

He bent to stroke Frankie's head. The dog was used to being around gunfire, but she had probably experienced some fear as well. "That's my girl," he said.

He put Frankie back in the kennel. The driver's-side door was bent and wouldn't open, so he crawled in through Lydia's side and then Lydia got in. The vehicle clearly needed to go to the body shop but maybe it would get them back to town.

The car made grinding noises as he backed it away from the tree. His side window was a spider web. Then he turned the wheel to drive up the slanted dirt incline. It took several tries of backing up and moving forward before the front tire on his side touched the pavement. He got back on the road, pulling his phone out and pressing Eva's number before he rolled forward.

"River, what can I do for you?"

"Can you find out who owns the land next to that hiking trail for me?"

"That should be easy enough. Those things are a matter of public record. I thought we were operating on the assumption that Elsie was taken away in that car."

"I'm just wondering if the guy that owns that land was out there and saw something," said River. "If you could send me a map of the area, as well, that would be good."

"Can do," said Eva. "I started the background check on Prentiss Grafton. He's gotten into a lot of altercations, most of them pled down to misdemeanors, but clearly a guy who doesn't have control of his temper."

River thanked Eva and Lydia pressed the disconnect button for him while he drove.

"Got to follow every lead, huh?" Her voice sounded faint. She was losing hope. The last nearly fatal encounter had taken a lot out of her.

"We're not giving up."

She rested her palm against her forehead then patted his leg with the other hand. "Thank you." After a long moment, she let out heavy breath. "Do you think that was the same man who came after me at my house?"

Though he had followed the attacker into the trees that night, River couldn't say much about him except that he was tall, maybe six foot. "Same build, I would say."

A voice came over the radio; the police officer who was his backup. "Officer Hanes here. I never caught up with the tan SUV. He kind of just disappeared. He must have turned off a side road but, honestly, I didn't see any. Kind of weird."

"Thank you for your effort." River put the radio back in the slot.

The downward spiral of despair was almost palpable in the car.

"At least we know the make and model of the SUV, and it's not looking good for Prentiss Grafton," said River.

He supposed the next step should be to get forensics up to the trail to try to retrieve the rifle brass. With the help of the task force and the local PD, he was working this case from every angle and yet they didn't seem to be getting anywhere. Elsie was still gone.

River stopped at the police station to leave the damaged patrol car to get repaired and to borrow another in the meantime.

The drive back to Lydia's house seemed unbearably long. He only hoped he could keep her safe from another potentially deadly attack.

SIX

Lydia felt utterly defeated as River pulled up in front of her house. The patrol car was no longer parked out front. "I'll stay with you until we can get another officer to stand watch. Let me call and find out when that will be."

As she sat next to him in the patrol car, Lydia only heard one side of the phone call, but it sounded like they were short of officers because of a bank robbery. He shut off his phone and turned to face her, blue eyes holding an intense warmth. "I can stay with you for now."

River got Frankie out of her kennel and escorted Lydia up the walk. She pulled her keys from her pocket. Once inside, River gripped her arm. "Let Frankie and me make sure this place is secure."

She watched as Frankie and River moved from room to room and then stepped outside into the backyard.

Lydia slumped down on the sofa and grabbed a picture frame from the side table. Elsie in her princess costume. She pressed the photograph to her chest and closed her eyes as they warmed with tears.

River returned.

"Hey." He rushed over to her and gathered her into his arms.

She nestled against his chest, resting her palm where she

could feel his heart beating. Frankie licked her hand. They were quite a team, these two.

"You don't find all the children, do you? You said there have been times when there wasn't a happy ending."

He pressed his warm hands against her cheeks and looked her in the eyes. "Lydia, you can't let your mind go there."

The tears flowed down her cheeks and over his fingers. "I just have to face reality. There are times when the search doesn't end well, aren't there?"

He pulled away. "Yes, there are bad outcomes sometimes." His voice was thick with emotion.

"What happened, River?"

He rose to his feet. He stared at the framed photo of Elsie then covered his mouth with his hand, shaking his head. "A five-year-old boy died on my watch. I didn't make the right choices." His voice faltered. "I should have asked more questions about the family situation." He turned his back to her, resting his head in his palm.

This had to be what he'd been keeping from her. The thing that tore him up inside. She stood and touched his back. He turned to face her. "No child will die on my watch ever again."

Even as she acknowledged the intense resolve in his eyes, she had to accept that regardless of River's vow, the outcome for a missing child could not be controlled. Lydia detected deep sorrow in River. It hadn't been easy for him to share. She gave him a sideways hug. "Oh, River, I'm so sorry. You didn't have to carry that alone."

He turned to face her. "You can't give up hope. Stay strong for Elsie and I'll stay strong for you. Deal?"

He was right. She couldn't give up hope. She had to believe that Elsie was alive and that she would be found. She tilted her head to look at him. "Deal." It would be so easy to fall for him. She took a step back. That look in his eyes made her fear he would kiss her again. This time on the lips. The pain of her marriage to Sloane flooded back over her. There was a reason she'd vowed to stay single.

She needed to keep her perspective. Maybe the strong feelings for River were just because of the way he'd risen to the occasion in the worst crisis of her life.

His phone rang. He looked at it. "Ah, Eva. She always comes through."

Lydia was grateful that the phone call broke the intensity of the moment. Was she just attracted to him because of the nightmare she was living through? She only heard one side of the phone conversation. "Gregory Larson, huh? What do you know about him and that land?"

River listened for a moment. "Yeah, give me the address. Let me get a piece of paper."

Lydia handed him a piece of paper and a pen from the sofa side table. River nodded while Eva talked. "Okay, still, it might be good to talk to him." He said goodbye and pressed the disconnect button.

Lydia took a step toward him. "What did you find out?" Again, she felt her hope rising. She didn't know how much more of this emotional roller-coaster ride she could take.

"Gregory Larson owns about forty acres next to the hiking trail," said River.

"I don't know why, but his name sounds familiar."

"He's made a lot of money in real estate and owns many properties around Ridge and sells all over the state."

"Maybe that's it." She'd probably seen one of his real estate ads.

"His house is on a different piece of property outside of town, but there's a private skeet shooting range and a structure that functions as a clubhouse on his land that's next to the hiking trail."

"We didn't see anything like that," said Lydia.

He looked again at his phone. "Eva's supposed to send me a map to show where the clubhouse is." He studied his phone for a long moment. "Looks like it's a couple of hills over. The boundary between the properties is right at that creek where Frankie and the other dogs lost the scent."

"So, it's not likely even if Mr. Larson was on that property that he saw anything."

"It might be worth it to talk to him. Maybe see if he would give us permission to search that clubhouse. It's probably only used when people are up there shooting."

Straws, thought Lydia. "In case Elsie was taken there and hidden? So, whoever took her hiked over two hills instead of taking her in the car that was seen at the time she disappeared?"

"I know it seems like Frankie would have followed the scent if she was taken that way. So much of this doesn't make sense. If I could just connect the dots." He threw up his hands. "With the rain and the creek, maybe it just distorted the scent too much." He wandered over to the window by the front door, gazing at the street with his arms crossed over his chest. "I just don't understand it."

She moved toward the stove. "I'm going to heat up some water for tea." She filled the teakettle and placed it on the burner before turning it on. Frankie let out low growl.

"What is it, girl?."

Taking a step back from the stove, Lydia turned to look at Frankie.

She heard three popping sounds and then an intense hot energy picked her up and threw her backward. The kettle hit her shoulder. Her back rammed against a piece of furniture and papers fluttered around her. There was a giant black spot where her stove used to be. Her heartbeat drummed in her ears as shock set in.

River was lifting her, telling her something she couldn't quite process. He all but carried her through the front door. Had a bomb just gone off in her house?

With his own heart pounding, River wrapped his arm around Lydia's waist and rushed her through the front door. Frankie followed him. Though the explosion had been small only damaging part of the kitchen, it would have killed her if she hadn't stepped away from the stove. Frankie's warning growl had saved Lydia's life.

He pulled his phone out.

He didn't even wait for the 911 operator to talk. "There's been an explosion at 407 Weston Street." He went down on one knee beside Lydia. "Are you okay? Are you hurt?"

She nodded. "I don't think anything is broken."

"Let's go sit in my patrol car." He was concerned that there might be another explosion. The outside of the house hadn't been damaged at all, but that didn't mean they were out of danger.

Frankie settled between them in the car. After a few minutes, River saw flashing lights and heard sirens approaching up the street. The fire truck pulled up first. They waited in the patrol car until the ambulance showed up.

River escorted Lydia toward a waiting EMT. Several of the firemen were walking around the outside of the house, but none had yet gone inside. One of them came toward River and Lydia.

"Can you describe exactly what happened?"

Lydia sat on the bumper of the ambulance and pulled the blanket the EMT had offered her around her shoulders.

"There were popping sounds right after I turned on my gas stove, then I was sailing through the air."

The firefighter put his hands on his hips. "We're concerned that there might have been a gas line explosion, which means there might be a gas leak. I'm not sending my guys in there until we know it's safe to enter."

"You mean there might be more explosions?" said River.

The fire chief turned back toward the house. "Looks like an old house. Was the stove recently installed? Have you had any work done recently?"

"No recent construction." Lydia shook her head. "I have to tell you that there have been other attempts on my life."

He stared at her for a long moment. "I'm not sure what's going on, but we'll figure it out." The fire chief walked toward one of the other firefighters.

Lydia clutched the blanket close to her neck. "My house. My things. Elsie's things." The strain in her voice was like a knife stabbing his heart. One more thing had been taken from her.

After the EMT checked her out, River rested his hand on her shoulder. "You're staying with me for now." Dropping her off at a friend's house might not be a good idea. At least with him, she'd be safe.

Lydia had a sort of dazed look on her face as she got into the passenger seat. River had loaded Frankie in the back seat.

"Do you ever feel like you're living Job's life? Now I can't live in my house because of some kind of freak accident… if that even is what it was."

Even if the explosion had been caused by a gas leak, he too wondered if it had been an accident or deliberate sabotage.

Either way, he wouldn't leave her alone, and he certainly

wouldn't let her spend the night at some hotel when she was this vulnerable. She'd come to his place, where he could offer her his protection. With only a little arguing from her end, she agreed. She weakly mentioned that she could stay with her in-laws, but she seemed worried about causing them more stress.

River drove through town. Fully aware that they might be followed, he checked his mirror and took a circuitous route to his house. They stopped at a discount department store so Lydia could get toiletries and a change of clothes. Because he'd just moved to Ridge, he'd rented a house.

The house was small but on a large lot with a fenced backyard for Frankie. He didn't have a guest room. The second bedroom was still filled with boxes. "You can sleep in my room. I'll sleep on the couch."

She glanced around at the bare-bones room. "Guess your favorite color is brown, huh?"

They both laughed. She put her newly purchased possessions on the bed.

"I need to let Frankie out so she can run around."

"I'll go with you," she said.

The backyard connected with a park that had playground equipment. On the other side of it were the backyards of other houses. An older woman working in her garden waved at River. Lydia sat in his one outdoor chair, and he sat on the steps while Frankie ran around.

"So, are you going to go talk to Gregory Larson?"

"Yes, but first I need to call Second Chances." He just couldn't let go of the idea that Sloane Caldwell was somehow involved. "We know Sloane was there the whole time, but maybe he had someone else helping him."

He pulled his phone out while Lydia picked up a ragged

rope toy and played tug-of-war with Frankie. It was late in the day. River hoped he could get hold of someone.

"Second Chances. How can I help you?"

He recognized the voice as the woman he had previously talked to. "This is Officer Jameson in Ridge. I spoke to you previously about Sloane Caldwell."

"Yes, I remember."

"I know that Sloane never left the facility at the time of Elsie's disappearance, but did anyone else?"

"We have runners all the time. Let me check the log." He could hear keys clicking and then she got back on the line. "We had a man, D. J. Ketterling, leave and not come back the night before the little girl's disappearance."

"Did he and Sloane know each other?"

"They had group therapy together, and I did see them eating together several times. I can't talk about what was said in therapy, but I think they bonded over feeling betrayed by their ex-spouses."

Maybe D.J. had felt such an affinity toward Sloane that he decided to do his dirty work for him. "His whereabouts are unknown?"

"At this point, yes," she said.

"What did he look like?"

"A blend-into-the-crowd kind of guy, short brown hair, no real distinct features, no tattoos. He was a fairly tall man, at least six feet."

River's ear perked up. Though it was not solid evidence, the fact that D.J. was tall, like the attacker, was interesting at the least. "Thank you." D. J. Ketterling probably had a record and would be in the system. River only needed to make a phone call to Eva to see if she could track him down. Maybe one of the task force members could go to his last-known address. River needed to stay close to Lydia.

Lydia laughed as Frankie tugged on the rope. She had a soft laugh like a babbling creek. It was good to see her relax enough to enjoy herself even if it was only a brief break.

River made the phone call to Eva and then they went inside. "Not sure what I have around here to eat. Maybe I can order us a pizza."

"Do you live on pizza?" Her voice held a teasing tone.

"Pretty much."

"Let's see what you got for food before we take the pizza option. I'm pretty good at coming up with recipes on the fly." She looked in the cupboards, the freezer and the refrigerator. She gathered tuna and pasta and then pulled a can of peas from the cupboard. "Now, if you have some cheese in the fridge, we'll be in business."

"All I got is the dried Parmesan. I don't have a lot of time to shop and things in the fridge tend to go bad before I use them, so I purchase things with a longer shelf life." He really hadn't put much of an effort into settling in. The police station felt more like home to him. Work had always been where he felt like he was in his element. A house was just a place to sleep.

"I'll make it work," she said. "A sort of modified tuna casserole."

He moved to grab a saucepan. "I'll get the noodles started."

There was something fun though about cooking with Lydia that made him start to like where he was living.

He turned on some music, and they cooked in companionable silence. Once the casserole was thrown together, he pulled a half-eaten bag of potato chips from the pantry. "They are BBQ."

She snagged the chips. "Let's live adventurously. We'll invent a whole new recipe."

Her enthusiasm made him smile. Playing with Frankie in the yard seemed to have taken away some of the fear and stress she was carrying.

She crumbled the potato chips on top of the assembled casserole. Lydia could even make fixing dinner fun. He could get used to this. He wondered how anyone could mistreat her like Sloane had. She put the casserole in the oven and turned to face him.

A faint smile graced her face. "What's the serious expression about?"

"I was just thinking that it must have been tough for you and Elsie when everything happened with your husband."

The smile faded from her face. "It was the death of a dream. My whole life, I wanted to be part of a happy family. I never really knew my parents, and my aunt did things out of a sense of duty. When we were dating, Sloane painted a picture that implied that a solid family was what he wanted, too. But it was all just talk. How about you? No plans for a wife and family?"

He shook his head. "I don't know. I'm kind of married to my job." Even more so since what had happened with Noah. He didn't tell her that after what had happened to Noah, he didn't feel like he deserved to have children in his life. If he couldn't keep one five-year-old boy safe, maybe he couldn't keep any child safe. "I have a sister with two little boys who live in Denver. I see them when I can."

They ate dinner and then River found a movie for them to watch, but Lydia seemed distracted preferring to pay attention to Frankie. Her mind was probably still on her daughter. Lydia's phoned buzzed that she had a text. Her face brightened and then fell when she saw who it was.

"It's Elsie's grandparents. They want to know if there's any news." She shook her head. "I had a moment of thinking it was someone telling me they'd found Elsie. I guess any time my phone rings, that will be my first thought."

He reached out, rubbed her back, and then drew her into a side hug. There was nothing he could say that would take away her anxiety. Best just to be with her. He turned off the movie since she hadn't been watching it anyway. His attempt to get her mind off Elsie's kidnapping had not worked.

Within twenty minutes, Lydia was asleep on the sofa. He placed a throw over her. With all that had happened, he was surprised that she hadn't collapsed sooner. River took Frankie and walked the perimeter of his house. He didn't think they'd been followed, but with all the attempts on her life, he couldn't take any chances where Lydia was concerned.

When he came back in the house, Lydia was no longer on the sofa. He had a second of panic until he saw the closed bedroom door indicating that she had gone to bed. He double-checked to make sure the doors were locked and the windows latched. He checked his phone. A text from Eva saying she'd gotten hold of Gregory Larson and that he had agreed to meet them on the land that connected with the trail where Elsie had disappeared. A thin lead at best, but he was running out of ideas.

River sat his gun on the side table and then lay on the sofa, pulling the blanket over himself. His plan was to get up and walk a patrol several times in the night. After all that had happened, he needed to remain on high alert. Maybe he could keep Lydia safe through the night, but Elsie was still out there somewhere…alive, he hoped.

SEVEN

Lydia awoke with a start. Her breathing was intense, as if she'd been jogging. Except for a night-light that illuminated Frankie sleeping on her bed in the corner, the room was dark and the shades were drawn.

Her heart was still pounding from the dream she'd had. She'd been running through the forest, calling for Elsie. As she'd moved through the trees, she could hear the little girl crying out for her, but Lydia could never see her. Then the dream shifted to the edge of the cliff—only it was Elsie falling down, screaming for Lydia. Instead of a deep canyon, the cliff turned into a black abyss where Elsie got smaller and smaller until she was eaten up by the darkness.

Frankie rose from her bed and trotted over to Lydia, placing her front paws on the bed.

She touched the dog's soft fur. "I'm okay. I just had a bad dream."

After throwing off blankets, she stepped into the bathroom to get a sip of water. The fear the dream had instigated still had not faded. She rested her hands on the vanity and stared into the sink. "It wasn't real, Lydia." Even taking a deep breath didn't help wipe the images from her mind. She closed her eyes.

Elsie is safe. Elsie is alive.

She prayed for God to quiet her racing thoughts. When she returned to the bedroom, she heard River moving around in the kitchen.

After grabbing the robe River had loaned her, she stepped into the open-concept living room and kitchen area.

River was still fully dressed. He stood in the kitchen, a steaming mug sitting on the counter. It looked like he couldn't sleep, either. "Everything okay?"

She stepped toward him. "I had a bad dream."

He met her gaze. "I guess I don't have to ask you what it was about."

"River, I'm so afraid for her. I can't stop thinking about it."

He reached out to her, and she fell into his arms. He repeated her name several times. She was grateful that he didn't offer empty assurances. Elsie's welfare and whereabouts were unknown. Lydia relished the warmth and safety of his embrace. As he held her, she realized giving in to the fear would make it that much harder to focus on what she could do to bring Elsie home safe.

After stepping away from the hug, she swiped at her eyes. "Guess I'll try to get a few more hours' sleep."

"In the morning, we'll go out and talk to the man who owns the land next to the hiking trail. When I talked to him, he said he wanted to help. He had no problem with us taking the dogs into that clubhouse he has close to his skeet shooting range."

She turned to face him. "Like you said, we have to work all the angles." She tried to sound upbeat.

He nodded. "I'm not quitting until we have answers."

His tenacity gave her strength to keep going. But they both knew that the answer might be that Elsie was no longer alive.

With doubt and hope wrestling in her mind, she retreated to the bedroom with Frankie, the self-appointed bodyguard, at her heels.

After she got under the covers, Frankie jumped up on the bed. The dog nuzzled close to her side. She stroked Frankie's fur. "You understand, don't you?"

With Frankie close, she drifted off to sleep, though the images and sounds of Elsie crying out as she'd fallen still echoed through her mind.

She awoke hours later when light streamed through the window. Frankie was still sleeping by her.

She stroked the dog's head. "Thanks for helping me get through the night."

Lydia got up, showered and changed into the clothes she'd bought at the store. She'd have to go back to her place to get more clothes at some point. She didn't have the income to keep buying new outfits.

When she stepped into the kitchen, River had changed. His blond hair was slicked back from his face. He tossed her a protein bar, which she caught. "Eat up. I heard from Gregory Larson's assistant. The only time he can meet with us out at that land is early this morning. Apparently, he's got a packed schedule dealing with the real estate business."

She pocketed the protein bar and headed toward the door. Within minutes, she was sitting in the passenger seat of River's patrol car as they headed out of town. Frankie sat in her kennel.

Tension knotted the back of Lydia's neck. She prayed they'd find something that would lead them to Elsie.

River kept his eyes on the road as he took the turn that would lead to the back side of the property Gregory Larson owned. He slowed down when the paved road turned to dirt.

"I've asked one of the other task force members to meet us up there. Lizzie has a K-9 who's trained to track. She was here for the initial search, the blond woman with the golden retriever. Two noses are better than one. I don't want to take a chance of missing anything if Elsie was anywhere near that clubhouse."

Any small morsel of evidence would help at this point.

If Elsie hadn't been taken away in that car, where else could she have been hidden? The kidnapper would have had to carry her over a hill. There had been plenty of brush and trees that would have hidden them from view. Still, he could not understand why Frankie and the other dogs had completely lost the scent at the creek. It was as if a helicopter had landed and taken Elsie up in the air.

The road he was on was different than the one that led to the trail or the one where the car had been seen. He took several more turns and then the clubhouse and the skeet shooting range came into view. When he checked his rearview mirror, he saw Lizzie's patrol vehicle behind him. Just having another task force member help out would lighten his load. The focus on finding Mia before it was too late and getting justice for the other three women had caused the members to bond quickly.

The road leveled off. River stopped his car and Lizzie parked beside him. Two men were at the shooting range. One operated the trap and the other aimed his rifle at the sky. Off in the distance, a man was flying a drone and two others were practicing fly-fishing casts. The land was used for more than just skeet shooting. The clubhouse was some distance from the range. It looked to be a prebuilt modular home that had been hauled in. River, Lydia and Lizzie all got out of their vehicles.

The man shooting skeet leaned his rifle against a stump

and walked toward them. River recognized him from ads. Gregory Larson was tall and in good shape. He was probably in his late thirties or early forties. As he got closer, River's assessment was that there was a fake quality to him. Gregory's tan was a little too even to have happened naturally by being in the sun and his blond hair had dark roots.

Gregory held out his hand. River made quick introductions.

"So sorry to hear about that poor little girl," said Gregory. He turned to Lydia. "This must be difficult for you."

Lydia managed a nod.

"I'll do anything to help." Gregory shifted his weight focusing his gaze on River.

"Were you on the land the day Elsie was taken?"

He shook his head. "I had a showing in Colorado Springs. Sorry I can't be of more help."

River glanced over at the men practicing their fly-fishing casts. "Looks like you use the land for other things. Do you know if anybody else was here?"

"I can ask around. People come and go as they please once they pay a small rental fee for the use of the land. Just trying to make this place pay for itself. The clubhouse is only opened for members of the skeet shooting club."

"If you don't mind, we'd like to deploy the dogs to see if there was any trace of the girl having been here," said River.

"Sure, I've left the clubhouse door unlocked. I've got to head out for a showing here in twenty minutes. The last person to leave will lock up for me."

Using Elsie's jacket, which Lydia had taken with her when she'd left her place, River and Lizzie deployed the dogs. While River headed toward the clubhouse, Lizzie directed Reena to work her way downhill. From the map he'd looked at, River knew the creek and the dirt road were two hills over from the clubhouse.

Lydia followed River and Frankie. The inside of the clubhouse was one big room with a large table and several couches and chairs, a bar near the kitchen had several stools by it. The counter had a coffee machine. The center of the room had a large fireplace that looked like it had never been used.

River looked around. "The electrical must be run on some kind of generator." If the fireplace wasn't being used, they must have another way to heat the place.

After River commanded her to search, Frankie put her nose to the ground and move around the room.

Lydia checked the two other doors that connected to the big room and then returned to the main room. "Just a bathroom and a storage closet with cleaning supplies and tools." She rubbed her arms. "I don't know why I thought I would find some evidence that she'd been here. She was wearing barrettes that day and a little beaded bracelet that I helped her make. She had on her floral windbreaker."

The look of distress on Lydia's face cut right through him. "All the same, let's let Frankie do a deep search."

River led Frankie through the side rooms. The K-9 circled each room but gave no hint that Elsie had been there.

He returned to the main room where Lydia sat on a couch, waiting for him. Her expression, the wide eyes and raised brows, held a question.

He shook his head.

Her shoulders slumped. When they stepped outside, Lizzie was headed up the hill with Reena. Gregory's car was gone, as was one of the men practicing his fly casting.

They walked toward Lizzie. "So sorry, Lydia, but Reena

couldn't pick up on any sort of scent. I went as far as the top of the hill where I could look down and see the creek."

As they loaded up and headed down the mountain, River felt like he was in quicksand. They were running out of angles to work. What had happened to that precious little girl?

Lydia's silence suggested she was in the same mental space as he was. What thread could he pull to make the case hot again? He refused to give up hope. He took his phone from his pocket and sat it on the console. "Press in Eva's number. Maybe she has come up with something."

Lydia picked up the phone and scrolled, pressing a number.

Eva's voice came through on speaker. "River, what's up?"

"Just wanted to check with you. Did all the background checks on the people at the school come back?" He swallowed and glanced in Lydia direction. "Wonder if you came up with anything."

"Give me a second. I just had my first sip of coffee, so I'm moving a little slow." River could hear keys tapping. "We're still waiting on a couple of background checks. So far, everyone but Prentiss Grafton is pretty clean. When I called him, he said he was out of town the day of Elsie's kidnapping. I still have to confirm his alibi. Give me a second, let me check the police reports I requested." There was a pause, as if Eva was reading, and then the keys tapped some more. "It seems that D. J. Ketterling's ex-wife called in a domestic the night before Elsie disappeared. D.J. showed up drunk, wanting to see his four-year-old son. The ex called the cops, and he fled the scene. The house is just outside of Ridge."

Elsie had been taken in the early afternoon of the next day. Plenty of time to get up to the trail or even to follow them from the school.

"No sign of D.J. since then?"

"No, the guy fell off the radar after that. He'd been evicted from the apartment he previously rented before he went into Second Chances. I'm trying to track down his known associates." Eva let out an audible breath. "River, I want to find this little girl as badly as you do, but the net we're casting is pretty wide. We've got to find a way to narrow things down."

"I know. Maybe I can question Sloane. It's a long drive to get to where he's at. Maybe there is something there. Even if he's not supposed to talk to anyone at this stage of his rehab, there are legal ways we can compel him to talk to us." He clenched his jaw. Time Eva spent helping with Elsie's case was time away from the baby snatching ring. "Give me a little more time. A strong lead has to come up somewhere."

"Hang in there." Eva's voice was fused with compassion. "I'll let you know if anything comes up on this end."

"Thanks, Eva." Her words, as kindly as she had spoken them, hung heavily in his mind.

Lydia pressed the disconnect button, a grim expression on her face.

"I think we need to look at your ex-husband again. Maybe he sent D.J. as his proxy. It sounds like Ketterling didn't have any visitation rights with his kid, either. Maybe they bonded over that. I just can't let go of the idea that your ex is involved. Did his drinking lead to illegal activity or associating with people on the wrong side of the law? Maybe someone wanted to get back at Sloane by hurting you and Elsie."

She shook her head. "It was just the DUIs that did him in and my telling the police he'd driven with Elsie in the car. There's no one who would come after Elsie and I for that reason."

River's throat went tight. His voice was soft. "I just don't know where else to look."

"How long before Elsie's case is considered a cold one?"

They had turned onto the paved road. Before he could answer, Lizzie, who had been driving ahead of them, radioed. “I’m headed back into Ridge. I’ll be around for a few hours if you need anything.”

“Got you,” said River.

He watched as she turned onto the road that led back into town.

Lydia glanced in the side mirror and then over her shoulder. “Oh no, we’ve got a problem.” Fear permeated her voice as she gripped the armrest.

River glimpsed the rearview mirror in time to see the tan SUV behind them, zooming toward his patrol car.

EIGHT

Lydia's heart pounded as the tan SUV got closer to their bumper. River pressed the accelerator to the floor then turned his head side to side, maybe trying to find a possible escape route.

He pulled the radio. "Lizzie. We're being chased. Could use some help."

"On it. Let me get turned around."

"I just turned on to the highway," said River.

The first hit to their bumper propelled Lydia forward in her seat. The seat belt dug into her flesh. Her heartbeat revved up.

The SUV zoomed forward, so its front was even with the back end of River's patrol car. The vehicle kept up with them as River increased his speed. The tan SUV sideswiped the patrol car, sending it off the road, then seemed to follow them from its position on the road, probably to take another shot.

The land was flat, bumpy, with trees in the distance.

"Unbuckle your seat belt and get down low." River glanced all around. "We got to play some defense here." He turned the wheel to head back to the road.

Lydia did what he said even though she wasn't sure what he had planned.

River performed a tight turn. She heard a banging noise as Frankie slid around in her kennel. The K-9 whimpered. River spun the car completely around then braked. He was using his car to block the road.

River had unbuckled his seat belt and pulled his gun. He pushed open his door, which was on the far side of the road, away from the tan SUV.

She lifted her head above the ledge of the passenger's-side window. The SUV was only yards away, the motor still running.

"Get down," said River.

A single shot was fired. Her heart raced as she squeezed herself into the space on the floor underneath the dashboard.

The momentary distraction had given River time to move to the hood of his car.

A volley of shots caused her to wince each time a round was fired.

A second later, River jumped back in the patrol car and pressed the gas. "He's getting away."

When she crawled back into her seat, Lydia could see the rear end of the SUV as River sped toward it. Just as River got close to the other vehicle, it suddenly turned onto a dirt road. River sped past, turned around and went back to the dirt road where the tan SUV had gone.

She saw Lizzie's patrol unit coming toward them as they turned. Once they were on the road where the tan SUV had gone, she spotted its taillights before it disappeared around a bend. Forest bordered them on both sides.

As they rounded another curve, she realized they were on the road that led to the border between the hiking trail and Gregory Larson's land. It was the road the car had been spotted on the day Elsie disappeared. She could see the forested hill, and beyond that was the hiking trail, but there was no sign of the tan SUV.

River slowed down. Lizzie caught up with them.

Lydia looked all around. "I don't see him anywhere." The road they were on came to a dead end. He couldn't have driven through.

River slowed the car. "He must have turned off somewhere."

She didn't remember seeing any roads that intersected with the one they were on. Maybe there had been an opening in the forest that would have provided a degree of cover.

Lizzie's voice came through on the radio. "Where did he go?"

"Not sure. I'm going to backtrack in the car. If you want to deploy Reena, maybe he hid the car somewhere and took off on foot."

While Lizzie got out of her SUV with her golden retriever, River backed his patrol car up until he could get turned around. They rolled along the dirt road slowly, both of them watching their respective sides of the road. The tan SUV would blend in with the trees. Still, unless the driver was able to go deep into the woods, it seemed like they would be able to spot it.

"If the guy abandoned his vehicle and took off running, Lizzie's dog would find the scent. When a person is afraid, which is the case anytime you are on the run, he or she emits a scent that the dogs can pick up on."

If that was what had happened, where was the SUV?

River activated his radio. "Anything?"

Lizzie's voice came through. "Nothing."

"Thanks for your help."

"No problem. I've got to get back into Ridge. I'm checking out the homes for unwed mothers to see if Gayle was seen at any of them."

"And to figure out if the home itself was used to facilitate the illegal adoptions?"

"That's one of the theories we're working with anyway. Those babies had to be born somewhere. I'll let you know if anything comes up. Emmett's probably going to want to do a video call soon. We've got task force members in Denver trying to figure out which free clinic Gayle may have gone to."

"Lots of channels of inquiry." River let out a heavy breath. "Something's got to turn up. Mia is out there somewhere."

Lydia picked up on the frustration in River's words. River struck her as a patient person. But two missing girls in separate cases and no progress on either was probably wearing on him.

Lizzie's words were a reminder to Lydia that River had another case he needed to be working on.

River spoke into his radio. "Hopefully something will lead us to Mia's whereabouts."

"Hopefully," came the other officer's response.

River put the radio back in its slot and drove toward the paved road.

"I know you have to get back to work on the task force investigation."

"Only if I can get an officer to watch my place. I'm not leaving you alone, Lydia."

They drove back into town to his house. River walked close to her, with Frankie on the other side of her, as they made their way up the walk.

Once they were at the door, River unlocked it. He squeezed her arm. "Stay just inside the doorway. Let Frankie and me clear the rooms before we go inside."

River wasn't taking any chances.

She turned and locked the door behind her while River and Frankie moved from room to room. Her phone rang. Sheryl. Lydia closed her eyes and pressed her palm against her chest. She dreaded having to give Elsie's grandmother the news that Elsie still had not been found.

"Sheryl, hello."

"I don't even need to ask. Your voice tells me everything. Sweet Elsie."

"She's out there. I feel it in my bones," said Lydia.

"How are you holding up?"

"Best as can be expected."

"Where are you? Norm went by your house and it was locked up."

She debated whether she should tell Sheryl about what had happened at her house. Sheryl's over-the-top reaction to every crisis tended to feed her own fear rather than calm her down. "The police thought it would be best if I didn't stay there."

"Norm wanted to drop off a gift card for food delivery. I'm sure the last thing you're thinking about is cooking. We want to help any way we can. Where are you at? He can bring them by for you."

"I appreciate that, but I'm all right. I have lots of time to cook. I'm in a safe place."

River came back into the room. Frankie trotted over to her, wagging her tail. "Mother Caldwell, I gotta go."

"You take care. Thoughts and prayers and all that."

"Thank you," said Lydia.

River held his phone in his hand. "Look, I've got to do a video call for the illegal adoption case. The team is all over Colorado chasing down every lead. Something's got to break here soon. Maybe Emmett has good news."

It was well past noon. "I can fix us some lunch."

"I don't have much in the way of food, but you worked your magic once before."

While River set up his laptop for the video call, she scoured the cupboards, coming up with a can of chili that she heated on the stove. The crackers she found looked a little stale. Maybe she should have taken up Sheryl's offer for Norm to drop off the gift card.

Then again, she doubted that River would think delivery people coming to his house and seeing her would be a good idea. Between the sparse contents in the cupboards and fridge, she couldn't come up with any more meal possibilities. The freezer held only one frozen pizza. They were going to have to go to the grocery store soon.

River sat his laptop on the kitchen table.

"Should I be listening to this meeting?" she asked.

"It's all right. Maybe you can give us a fresh perspective."

Lydia dished up the chili. When she brought the bowl over to River, only one woman's face was on the screen. She had dark hair and a bright smile.

Lydia returned to get her own bowl and wash her hands.

"Hey, Eva," said River.

"I'm glad you're early to the meeting. Saves me having to call you. It's about D. J. Ketterling."

"Yes. You have news?"

Wiping her hands on a towel, Lydia stepped closer to the computer.

"He was found dead down by a warehouse that was known to be a drug hangout."

"An overdose?" River's shoulders slumped.

Eva nodded. "The coroner estimated that he'd been dead for at least a day. That means he was dead at the time of Elsie's kidnapping."

Lydia felt like the walls were closing in on her. She slumped down in a chair beside River.

"I'm so sorry," said Eva.

Another dead end.

"I'm still working on verifying Prentiss Grafton's alibi," said Eva. "If he's not telling the truth, he's your prime suspect."

Before River could even process Eva's news, two more faces appeared on the screen. Emmett, his boss, and Maren, who had helped him track down the father of Gayle's baby. He reached over and gripped Lydia's hand where it rested on the table. The news about D. J. Ketterling had hit her hard.

Three more faces popped up on the screen. Autumn, Eli and Lizzie. Autumn Riley, who was a handler for Bear, a bloodhound trained in tracking and cadaver detection, was engaged to the half brother of Jenny Clarke, the first victim of the adoption ring. She'd been found murdered in Canyon Creek. Eli Blackwood had red hair and a beard. His Belgian Malinois, Wrangler, was trained in suspect apprehension. Some years ago, Eli's wife and infant daughter had been killed.

A final face came on the screen. Melody Rust. A redheaded officer with hazel eyes who lived in Boulder, she specialized in bomb detection with her male chocolate Lab, Dusty.

Emmett spoke up. "First of all, team, I want to thank you all for your diligence. Some of you have been going above and beyond in terms of the amount of time and mileage you've put into this investigation." The dark-haired task force leader seemed to take them all in with his blue-eyed gaze in one sweep.

River felt a pang of guilt. His ability to help move the case forward had been hindered by the time he'd put into finding Elsie. Mia needed saving, too. His heart twinged thinking of the missing pregnant teen. Her family—in particular, her grandfather Dodger, who'd helped form the task force to investigate her abduction—wanted the young woman found.

Emmett continued. "We're combing the state for every possible lead, including visiting homes for unwed mothers. River uncovered that Gayle may have gone to a free clinic in Denver. We have task force members down there, showing her photo as well as the ones of the other two girls, Jenny and Nina. There has to be a connection somewhere, a method and a means as to how these girls were found and taken hostage until their babies were born."

Autumn piped up. "I had a chance to visit two of the homes for unwed mothers. None of them remembered Gayle. Honestly, both places seemed aboveboard. I still have a couple more clinics to visit." River had spent time with Autumn last month checking out the homes and hospitals near Canyon Creek where Jenny Clarke had disappeared.

"One of the aspects of this case that we need to consider is not only how and where the girls are being targeted but how the adoptions unfold. We don't think this is happening through a legitimate agency. Eva has an update on what she's uncovered so far."

Eva brushed a strand of dark hair behind her ear. "Thanks, Emmett. As Emmett said, we don't think these adoptions are happening in any aboveboard agency. I got to thinking it has to be something online on the dark web. Maybe parents who are desperate for a child and willing to pay big bucks. They may or may not be aware that they are engaging in illegal activity."

Maren spoke up. "The desire for a child sometimes can

just be so strong that people don't see the red flags to think to do a little research about who they're dealing with."

"True," said Eva. "I've infiltrated a private online group on the dark web of parents seeking to adopt. We are looking at one couple in particular: Erin and Edward McGrath. They put an announcement in the Canyon Creek paper when they adopted their baby."

Autumn leaned closer to the screen. "Canyon Creek is where Jenny's body was found."

"Exactly," said Emmett. "We began the process of investigating them when they disappeared with their baby. We think they may have fled the country."

"That seems suspicious." Eli shifted in his chair. "Do you think the baby they adopted might be Jenny's?"

"It's a possibility. The birthdate corresponds."

"I interviewed a few of Erin and Edward's relatives, neighbors and coworkers," Melody interjected. "They all said the same thing. That the adoptive parents were very vague about how and where they had adopted the baby boy from."

"Maybe they knew or suspected the adoption agency wasn't legit," said River.

"I agree," said Emmett. "It makes them look guilty. We're going to try to track them down. In the meantime, our focus is on these clinics and the homes where the girls may have stayed. Eva will continue to snoop around the dark web adoption site. We may set up some sort of sting operation in the future with a fake couple wanting to adopt."

"River, how are things going with finding Elsie?" Autumn queried.

Eva's expression grew grim.

River could feel the heaviness in the room as Lydia sat next to him, out of sight from the people on the screen.

She'd been taking small bites of chili but mostly staring off into space.

"Eva's been helping me quite a lot. I know that's a drain on our resources," said River.

"Elsie life matters, too," said Eli. "As much as Mia's. We all feel the weight of what Elsie's mom must be going through."

"We got a guy from the school whose alibi still needs to be confirmed." He reached over and cupped his hand over Lydia's. "We're not giving up."

"Let us know any way we can help," said Autumn.

Several other task force members offered similar sentiments. River appreciated the show of support.

"River, when you have time, Eva dug up several more names of people who knew Gayle," said Emmett.

Tension threaded through River's torso. He wasn't carrying his weight in this investigation. Just as with Elsie's case, every lead could reveal where Mia was. "Sure. Eva, can you text me the names, addresses and relationship to Gayle?"

He watched Eva nodding on camera.

"River, I'll be in the area for a while if you need help." Maren offered him a smile that showed her dimples.

"Thanks," said River.

Emmett signed off and the faces disappeared from the screen one by one. Feeling torn, River stared at the black screen.

"Your chili's cold. Do you want me to reheat it for you?"

He'd only taken a few bites. "I can finish it this way, that's fine." The look on Lydia's face was so sweet, so trusting.

She picked up her empty bowl and took it over to the sink. She rested her hands on the counter with her back to him. "You have to get back to your job, don't you?"

He rose and came to stand beside her. She turned to face

him, green eyes filled with pain. "You saw how the team is. They want to find Elsie as bad as I do, but yes, a young woman's life is at stake."

"I appreciate everything that you've done for me, for Elsie." She reached up and pressed her hand against his forearm.

Her touch warmed him to the bone as guilt washed through him. He couldn't be in two places at once. "I won't leave for those interviews until an officer is parked outside."

"Thank you." Her expression softened and he found himself leaning closer to her, searching the depths of her eyes. He really wanted to kiss her.

She was the first to break the connection and step away. "Guess I'm staying here for the long haul. I don't know why I thought Elsie would be back in my arms by now."

He swept his thumb over her hand, still placed on his arm. "I know there's not much food in this house. Maybe after I get done today, we can get some groceries."

"I'd love to cook you a nice meal as a way of saying thank you."

Even in the middle of the biggest trial of her life, she was thinking of others. "I'd like that."

She turned back toward the sink to rinse out her bowl. "I hate to be a bother, but I need more clothes. I don't have a budget to keep buying them."

"It's not a bother. Maybe tonight, after I get back, I can take you to your place to grab a few more things."

"I'll call the fire department today and make sure it's safe to go back in," she said.

By the time River finished his chili, a female police officer was parked outside. He headed toward the door with Frankie beside him. This would be a long, lonely day for Lydia.

"Stay. Sit," he commanded. "I'm leaving her here. She'll keep you company and be an extra measure of protection."

"I appreciate that." Lydia walked over to touch Frankie's head.

Feeling torn between two devastating situations, River stepped outside alone. He waved at the officer behind the wheel.

Lydia stood at the window with Frankie resting her paws on the sill so she could see out.

He prayed for her safety as he got into his patrol car and pulled away from the curb.

NINE

Headlights from a car woke Lydia from where she slept on the couch with Frankie curled around her feet. Though she understood why she needed to stay in the house, she had made phone calls in an attempt to bring her daughter home. She called the school to find out if anything might have happened with Elsie that she hadn't known about. She called friends from church and the play group she and Elsie went to see if they had any ideas about who might have taken her little girl. All of it had led nowhere and left her exhausted.

She'd also called the fire department to get the okay to return to her house for clothes. The chief had said that it was safe for her to go back inside. He told her it looked like a gas leak but only an arson investigator would confirm if it had been accidental or on purpose.

She rose to her feet and walked over to the window. At well past eight, it was dark outside. She flicked on the porch light to see River was coming up the walkway holding a pizza box.

As she moved to unlock the door, the other officer pulled away from the curb. She opened the door.

River held up the pizza box. "I didn't figure you'd want to be cooking dinner this late. Maybe after you have a full belly, we can grab some groceries."

She smiled at him. "I see you prepared your specialty."

Her stomach growled. She'd found only a can of peaches with a questionable expiration date to snack on while she'd waited for River's return. He flipped open the box, allowing the scent of Italian spices and pepperoni to swirl around the room.

They sat down to eat after grabbing plates and napkins. "Did you learn anything from the interviews you did?"

"Mostly just confirmed stuff we already knew. That Gayle was alienated from her family, that she was a hard worker at the jobs she had. One of the people I talked to in the apartment where she lived said that she had also mentioned going to a clinic in Denver. He thought the clinic was affiliated with a major hospital, so that might help us narrow it down."

"That's something anyway." She took a bite of the gooey pizza.

He nodded. "Maren and I drove out to a home for unwed mothers outside of town. The place seemed legit." They finished their pizza.

After they cleaned up, River and Lydia got into his private car, leaving the patrol unit parked outside, so they could get groceries. He'd loaded Frankie in the back seat.

Lydia settled into the passenger seat just as her phone rang. It was not a number she recognized. "Hello?"

"I saw your daughter. The one who's been on the news."

Her heartbeat thrummed in her ears as she gripped the phone tighter.

River must have picked up on the intense shift in her emotional state. He leaned closer to her. She pressed the speaker button. Her throat had gone dry. "You know where my daughter is?"

"I saw her walking with a guy on Catron Street over by that abandoned apartment building."

"How long ago was this?"

"Three minutes ago."

"Who...who is this?"

"This is not a safe neighborhood and people don't like snitches." The line went dead.

The numbness and the sense that she was floating washed over her again. "We have to go. It was just three minutes ago." She gripped River's arm. "I know the police get anonymous tips all the time from people who just want attention or who really want to help but are mistaken. But we have to go. We have to check it out."

River started his car and handed her his phone. "Call Maren and see if she's still in the area. Then call the police."

She appreciated that River didn't question the validity of the call. His response was decisive.

"The police showing up might scare whoever has her away." She was already scrolling through his phone.

"You might be right about that, but I'm not going over there without backup."

"I know." She pressed in a number.

Maren answered on the first ring. "River, what's up?"

"This is Lydia Caldwell. Are you still close to Ridge?"

"Yes, I was just filling my gas tank before heading out."

Lydia swallowed and took in a breath. Her words came out in a staccato beat. "I just got a call that someone spotted Elsie on Catron Street by the abandoned apartment building. River and I are headed over there now."

Maren sounded breathless, as if she were running. "I'll get over there as fast as I can."

River cut in, leaning toward the phone as Lydia held it.

"If you're in your patrol car, hang back and walk in. An obvious police presence could put Elsie in danger."

"Got it," said Maren.

River drove through town. Every red light seemed to last forever. He slowed as the houses and buildings started to look more run-down. One man walked by himself along the street. The glow of televisions came from inside apartment building windows.

She could see the abandoned apartment house up ahead on a large lot with overgrown trees and bushes. River came to a stop by a car that had had its tires and bumper removed. She spotted a lone dog heading up the sidewalk, stopping to sniff something on a lawn. Tension coiled in her stomach as she drew her attention back to the boarded-up windows of the apartment building.

River pressed a number on his phone. "Where are you at?" He listened for a second then hung up. "She's working her way up the street with Haven. Her dog is trained in suspect apprehension."

Her gaze traveled up the three-story building to the top floor where some of the windows were not boarded. She jerked in her seat. "There—I saw a light in that corner apartment."

River pulled his gun. "Stay here."

She could see Maren with Haven less than half a block away, staying in the shadows the overhang of the buildings provided.

River got out of the car and let Frankie out of the back seat. He made his way toward the building. When he tried the ground-floor door, it swung open. He waited for a few seconds until Maren and Haven were a few yards from the door before going inside. The darkness enveloped both officers and their dogs.

Lydia looked again at the place where she'd seen a flash of light. The corner window remained dark. Her gaze rested on the overgrown trees and bushes that surrounded the building. This place had probably been quite nice in its heyday. Her eyes caught on a bit of color in a bush close to the sidewalk. She gasped.

No, it couldn't be. It looked like Elsie's little floral windbreaker. The one she'd been wearing the day she disappeared. Her heart was pounding as she opened the car door. When she glanced around, there was no one within three blocks of the building.

Compelled by the need to find her daughter, Lydia rushed toward where she thought she'd seen the flower print. She stepped off the sidewalk and reached through the overgrown bush. The fabric was soft in her hands. She blinked several times. It *was* Elsie's jacket.

The building remained dark and quiet. If she called River, it might alert the kidnapper and risk Elsie being harmed. She could barely get a breath. Her daughter was in that building.

Still clutching the windbreaker that smelled like Elsie, she moved to return to the car. The jacket had been low enough on the branch that it may have been dropped. She stopped. But it could've been planted, too.

Hands grabbed her and pulled her back into the deep labyrinth of trees. She didn't have time to let out a scream before a hand went over her mouth. She could feel herself being dragged deep into the tangle of undergrowth. She couldn't see the street anymore.

The force that held her was strong. She kicked her feet and twisted her body while clawing at the hand that suctioned over her mouth. The man threw her on the ground. When she landed on her back, she tried to sit up, but his hands went around her neck before she could cry out. She fought for breath as his thumbs pressed on her breathing tubes. The night got even darker as her vision was reduced to a pinhole. She scratched his hands, which made him press harder. She gasped for air.

She could hear pounding footsteps on the sidewalk. A dog barked.

The man dropped her on the ground, kicking her once in the side before running through the trees toward the back of the apartment building. Lydia curled up from the pain. Maren rushed past her with Haven right beside her.

A second later, River was by her side. He gathered her into his arms. Frankie licked her cheek. “You all right?”

“I guess.” The impact of the push and then being kicked had knocked the wind out of her. She’d hit the ground hard. Her back hurt. “Her coat.” She turned to the side where she’d dropped Elsie’s jacket. She gathered it close to her body. “This is Elsie’s. She wore it the day she disappeared.”

“It was a trap to get you here so he could have another crack at you.”

“He’s the one who has her.” The windbreaker was close to her nose. It smelled like her daughter, a mixture of honey and milk. She started to cry. Who had her baby? And was she hurt? When would she see her daughter again?

River took her in a tighter embrace. “Let’s get you back to the car.”

Still holding on to the coat, her knees felt weak. River wrapped an arm around her waist and helped her walk. Once she was secure in the passenger seat, he phoned the police. “There’s a man fleeing in the two hundred block of Catron Street. A K-9 officer is in pursuit on foot. Can we get some more units in the area…thanks.”

Lydia still hadn’t caught her breath. She breathed in the

scent of Elsie coat while the soft fabric brushed her cheek. "He's the one. He has her."

"Did you get a look at him?"

She shook her head. "It all happened so fast. He meant to kill me. Why?" Holding the coat gave her hope. Elsie was alive.

River's phone rang. "Maren?"

Lydia could hear Maren shouting something through the phone.

A dark figure emerged from the trees just as River put his hand over her and pulled her down. A single shot came through the window.

River ducked, pushing Lydia down as the shot rang out. A moment later, still draping a protective arm over Lydia, River raised his head above the dashboard. The windshield was spider-webbed but not broken. He could just make out the dark figure darting up the street, away from the occupied apartment buildings. After getting out of the car, he opened the back door and commanded Frankie to jump out. He made sure Lydia was safely locked inside, then drew his gun and took off running.

When he looked over his shoulder, Maren and Haven had come out of the trees by the building. His feet pounded the asphalt, which was uneven and in need of repair. He could no longer see the man who had just taken a shot at them, so he ran in the direction the attacker had gone.

He'd probably doubled back because his car was somewhere around here hidden from view. The attacker had seen his chance to take a shot at Lydia and fired a single bullet.

River passed a dilapidated house that clearly had not had anyone living in it. He slowed down. He couldn't see any movement anywhere, nor did he see a vehicle parked where the street came to a dead end and butted up against some overgrown bushes. The pounding footsteps behind him told him that Maren was close.

"You go that way," he shouted, pointing toward the bushes as he made his way through the falling-down fence that surrounded the abandoned house. The door creaked when he pushed it open. Frankie was one pace ahead of him. She let out a low-level growl.

His feet seemed to echo on the worn floorboards as he moved past the stairway through the living room to what must be the kitchen.

A sound above him caused him to tilt his head. Frankie let out a yip. The sound wasn't footsteps, more of a scurrying. A mouse maybe.

He stepped into the kitchen. He heard one abbreviated creak of the floorboards and then an object hit him in the back. A second blow knocked him to his knees. The gun fell from his hand. Frankie barked wildly.

He heard retreating footsteps. Before he could get back to his feet, Frankie was moving toward the door they'd just come through. He grabbed his gun where it had fallen and bolted outside.

The attacker was going to take another shot at Lydia.

When he stepped outside, River saw the man only feet away from his car. The attacker took three shots at the passenger's-side window, then darted up the street toward the occupied buildings.

River could barely take in a breath as he sprinted for his car with the shattered passenger window.

Maren and Haven emerged from the bushes. She must have heard the shots. "That way." He pointed up the street.

He needed to get to Lydia.

Please, God, don't let her be dead.

TEN

Glass had fallen on Lydia from where she'd crouched on the floor of the passenger seat when she'd seen the man running back toward River's car.

River reached in through the broken window and unlocked the door. "You're okay."

She looked up at him. After he opened the door, she crawled out of the cubbyhole that had saved her life. River wrapped his arms around her.

"I was so afraid for you." His voice washed with a measure of relief and joy.

"I was scared, too." She closed her eyes and rested her palm on his chest, appreciating the strength of his arms around her and the gentle cadence of his voice.

She was surrounded by his warmth and the rhythm of his breathing. If only she could stay there, forever safe in River's arms. She opened her eyes to the darkness and decay of the street around her. Back to reality.

He glanced up the street. "Not sure what's happening with Maren, but we need to get you out of here."

The chill night air surrounded her when she pulled away from the hug.

He glanced through the open door of the passenger seat. "There's a lot of glass in there. Why don't you sit in the back seat with Frankie?"

She reached in and grabbed Elsie's floral jacket while River loaded up Frankie. The dog pressed close to her. Frankie's warmth and soft fur and the sound of the dog's breathing had a calming effect on Lydia. She held the windbreaker close.

In the front seat, River phoned Maren, who assured him she'd called in the shooting. "Okay, thank you for the help. You put in a long day… Have a safe drive home."

She stared at the back of River's blond head. "She lost him?"

"Yes, his car was parked in the busier part of this street in a parking lot. She was on foot when she saw the tan SUV pull out."

She clutched the coat even tighter. "Why does he want me dead?"

"Not sure what's going on here." River rolled through the residential part of town and pulled out onto a street where there were businesses and neon lights. "That was quite a bit of glass that rained on you. Do you want to swing by the ER to be checked out?"

She looked at her hands and then touched her face. When she ran her fingers over her auburn hair, bits of glass fell out. The memory of the assault made her shudder. "I'm not bleeding. I just want to go home…back to your place."

"We were on our way to get food and clothes before all this happened. Are you up to it?"

Fatigue settled into her muscles. "I don't want to go back to my house. Let's just grab some food."

He drove to a box store that had food as well as clothes for sale. River stayed close to her as they entered the store together. She sensed that he was still on high alert. He'd checked his mirrors constantly while driving. He was expecting another attack.

After they got enough food for a couple days and a few items of clothing, River drove back to his house.

Once inside the house, he handed her the bag of groceries he'd been carrying. "Frankie and I are going to do a walk around the perimeter of the house. Why don't you try to get some sleep?"

She nodded. After putting the groceries away, she collapsed on the bed, placing Elsie's jacket on the pillow beside her. She rested her hand on the floral fabric and closed her eyes. Her mind raced. The logical part of her brain knew it was possible that Elsie was no longer alive. But her heart told her that Elsie was still out there somewhere. The kidnapper had known seeing the jacket would lure Lydia out of the car. Why she and Elsie had been targeted, she could not fathom. She closed her eyes and prayed for peace and for wisdom.

By the time she heard River and Frankie come back into the house, she felt herself drifting off to sleep.

Elsie, where are you?

She awoke to the sound of her phone ringing. Angel, her co-teacher.

"Oh, Angel, I'm so sorry. I meant to check in with you. There's just been so much going on."

"No worries. That's not why I'm phoned this morning. The class is running just fine. Your lesson plans are very detailed, and the parents have really stepped up to help in the classroom. We'll be fine in the short term."

"That makes me feel better. So, why are you calling?"

"It's Miles. He's still insisting that he saw an old lady with white hair in the trees the day Elsie disappeared. I know he likes to embellish and outright make things up for attention. But this feels different. Usually, he tells a story and then he's on to the next tall tale. He won't let go of this one."

"Maybe it would be worth it to have a police officer talk to him again," said Lydia.

"The reason I called this morning is that his mother is volunteering today, so she could sit with Miles while he's questioned."

"It might be good if I came along, too, since he trusts me." Lydia knew Miles well enough that she thought she might be able to discern if he was telling the truth, a half-truth, or just making the whole thing up.

"That sounds good. If you can come when the class is on their outside break or at the library, you can use the classroom."

"We'll get over there as fast as we can." After showering and changing into the clothes she'd bought the night before, she stepped into the kitchen where River sat at the table sipping coffee, Frankie at his feet.

"River, I have another straw that we can grasp at."

River looked up from his coffee. Lydia seemed to have regained some of her natural determination. "I'm willing to try anything at this point. I just heard from Eva that Prentiss Grafton's alibi checks out."

"Oh." Disappointment colored Lydia's features. "Then what I am about to tell you may be our only hope. That was my co-teacher on the phone. Miles, a boy who's in Elsie's class, keeps insisting that he saw an old woman in the trees the day Elsie was taken. He tends to make stuff up, but Angel says this feels different. Usually, if he's challenged about a tall tale he's told, he'll back down."

"I remember you mentioning that. Let's go over there and question the child." Without any strong leads, he'd been thinking of circling back to Sloane. Though an in-person interview would be best, the rehab was a three hour drive away. Talking to Miles might turn up the lead they needed. One of the things he'd learned about investigations was that when they stalled out, it was often worth it to revisit old evidence to try to see it with fresh eyes.

They both grabbed a protein bar and headed out the door with Frankie. They got into his patrol car. His personal car with the broken window was parked on the street. He'd have to get it into a window replacement place before he used it again.

He drove across town and parked in front of the school where Lydia taught. A group of children were playing outside.

"I'll call Angel to let her know we're here so she can have Miles and his mom go to the classroom where we'll have some privacy. The other kids will be in the library for forty-five minutes."

He deployed Frankie. The Lab's charm often worked well to build trust and break the ice when it came to asking questions of someone. It should work especially well with a four-year-old boy.

As they walked the halls, several teachers and a child came up to give Lydia a hug and ask her if there was any news of Elsie.

Lydia managed an answer, though her voice held a degree of strain and her features hardened as she spoke. The questions were coming from a place of genuine concern but repeating over and over that Elsie was still missing was clearly a struggle for her.

Lydia led River and Frankie to the empty classroom where a boy with brown curly hair sat with his mom. The room itself was decorated with children's art and educational posters in bright primary colors. Though River had only known Lydia since Elsie had been taken, the positive atmosphere of the room seemed to hint at who she had been before this tragedy. He pictured her at the beginning of the school year decorating the room for her kids.

Miles's eyes brightened when he saw Frankie. He got up from his chair. "Can I pet your dog?"

Frankie wagged her tail.

Works every time.

Miles stroked Frankie's head. "Her fur is so soft. Why does she have this vest on?"

Lydia got down to Miles's level. "Frankie is a police dog."

River got on his knees as well. "She's my partner, Miles. I'm a police officer."

Miles's mother piped up. "Why don't you come and sit back down, honey? Mrs. Caldwell and this nice policeman would like to ask you some questions."

Miles did a half twirl before sitting in his child-sized chair. "Is this about Elsie?"

"Yes." When River sat in one of the child-sized chairs, his knees nearly hit his chin. Frankie moved so she was in between River and Miles.

Miles stared at the table then stroked the dog's back. "I miss Elsie. She was my painting buddy."

"We all miss her." Lydia's voice swelled with emotion.

"Miles, I understand you saw a lady in the trees the day Elsie went missing."

Miles put his hands on his hips. "I told Miss Angel that."

"He mentioned it at home, too," said Miles's mother.

It sounded like the boy had been talking quite a bit about what he'd witnessed. "What can you tell me about the woman you saw?" River asked.

Miles pressed his lips together and wrinkled his forehead then he stared at the ceiling. "I talked about it already." He looked at River. Maybe he was hesitant to talk around a police officer.

Lydia rose from the chair and grabbed crayons and paper from a nearby table. "Maybe it would help if Miles drew a picture of what he saw. Miles is quite a good artist."

The boy grinned and raised his chin as she set the paper and crayons down in front of him. He chose a green crayon from the box and began to draw what looked like triangular evergreens.

At the same time Miles started drawing, he began to talk. Lydia's move had worked.

"She was an old lady with white hair." His finger traced the outline of the trees. "When we sat down to eat our snack, I was looking at the forest and everyone else was facing the trail. Miss Angel made me turn around."

"I do remember that." Lydia's voice brightened. "Miles likes to be different from the other children."

The little boy grinned and started to pet Frankie again. "Yup, that's me."

River put his finger on the trees. "This is where you saw the old lady?"

"Just a second." Miles selected several different colors and proceeded to draw ten circles. Then he turned them into faces and added details.

River didn't want to interrupt, but he needed to pick the kid's brain about what he'd seen in the trees.

Lydia shifted in her chair. "Miles, could you draw the old lady first?"

"Just a second," said Miles. He drew another circle covered in curly hair, with no face. "This is me."

Lydia gave River a raised eyebrow.

Miles's mother leaned close to him. "Honey, I think what they most want to know about is the lady that you saw."

Miles lifted his crayon from the page and crossed his arms. Clearly, he didn't appreciate that his creative process had been interrupted.

"Do you remember anything else about the lady? Was it just her white hair that made you think she was old?"

"No, she had an old face, too." He continued to pet Frankie.

Lydia pushed one of the crayons toward him. "Maybe you could show us."

River doubted that a drawing from a four-year-old would be lifelike, but the process of crayoning seemed to unlock some part of the kid's memory.

Miles picked up the crayon and drew a circle between the trees. "Her head popped up. She looked at where we were sitting. But I'm the only one who saw her."

"Yes, Miles. You are the only one," said Lydia.

The notion that he was special made the four-year-old smile again. He put a face on the circle.

"Anything else you remember about this woman?" said River. "What was she wearing?"

"I only saw her head just for a second. She went back in the forest where Elsie went to chase the butterfly."

River shifted on the tiny chair. "That's all?"

"That's all." Miles put his crayon down. His expression changed as something across the room drew his attention and he popped up from his chair. "Hey, wait a minute here." He walked across the classroom and picked up a white hat that had been put on a doll propped in the corner of the room.

Lydia turned in her chair. "Miles, what is it?"

He held the hat in his hands and stared at it. "Now I remember."

He waved the hat around. "Her hair wasn't white. She was wearing a white hat just like this one. The one Miss Caldwell wore for silly hat day."

"Just like that one?" All the color had drained from Lydia's face as she spoke in a monotone.

River wondered what had caused the sudden drop in mood. What had Lydia realized?

When Miles mentioned the hat, River thought he was adding to what might be a true story, but Lydia's reaction told him something else was going on.

River turned so he could look directly at Miles. "So, if her hair wasn't white, what color was it?"

Miles sucked on his finger and then pointed it at River while he stood on one foot. "I remember. It was kind of brown but not brown-brown." He riffled through the crayon box, holding up a ginger-colored crayon. "Like this." Miles proceeded to put hair on his circle and then drew the hat.

So maybe the woman's hair was strawberry-blond. Growing more agitated, Lydia laced her fingers together.

Miles pointed at his chest. "I'm telling a true story."

"Yes, you are. Miles, thank you." River nodded toward Miles's mother. "Thank you for letting us talk to your boy."

"Can I go be with the others in the library now? I'm going to find a book about cars."

"Sure," said River.

Miles put the hat down on the table by Lydia. He handed River the picture he'd drawn. "You can keep this."

"Thank you, Miles," said River.

After petting Frankie a few more times, he took his mother's hand and left the room.

Lydia picked up the hat and stared at the wall.

He scooted his chair closer to her. "Lydia, something Miles said shocked you. What is it?"

"This hat that I wore for silly hat day..." She turned so she could look directly at him. "My mother-in-law has one exactly like it. We bought it when we took Elsie to a craft fair." She let out a sharp breath. "River, what if Elsie's grandparents are involved in all this?"

ELEVEN

Lydia felt lightheaded as she rose from the chair. She could not fathom that her in-laws might have taken Elsie. How was it possible? Had they been in Grand Junction with Sloane's sister the day Elsie disappeared, like they'd said, or was that a lie? "I need to leave here." She was having a hard time getting a deep breath.

Frankie pressed close to Lydia and wagged her tail. She reached down to pet the yellow Lab. River escorted her through the building and opened the passenger's-side door for her. There were no children outside. Something about empty playgrounds always made Lydia sad.

Once they were settled in the patrol car, River spoke in a soft voice. "Lydia, I have to ask you some questions. Matching hats is not a slam dunk as far as evidence goes."

"I understand. I don't want it to be true," she said.

"So, you bought the hat at a craft fair. I assume that means it wasn't something that was mass produced?"

"The seller only had two handmade white hats. I bought the one with pink trim and Sheryl got the one with green trim."

"Do you think Sloane could put them up to taking Elsie?"

Feeling even more agitated, she massaged her temples. "They love their granddaughter. I let them visit her any time they want. They come to her school events. Why would they do something like this?"

"That's what makes me wonder if your ex-husband is behind this. Maybe he put them up to it."

"Maybe." She fiddled with her necklace, becoming more agitated as she spoke. *How could this be?* "They have a blind spot where their son is concerned. They might comply with a plan he cooked up." She shook her head. "Honestly though Norm is the one with the stronger personality. He's a high achiever, and he expected the same of his son. I often thought the pressure of those expectations was one of the things that led to Sloane's drinking."

"It's hard to understand family dynamics," said River.

"The bottom line is even if they were chilly toward me, they were always good to Elsie. I wasn't about to cut them out just because of Sloane's problems. I wanted her to have family in her life."

"Sloane was pretty angry about you getting full custody?"

"Yes, he was furious." She nodded. "She could have died that night in the car with him. He just didn't want to take responsibility. This latest rehab was court ordered."

"The first thing we need to do is check out their alibi. We don't want to talk to the daughter they went to visit, she might clue them in that we are looking into their whereabouts when Elsie was taken. There are other ways to verify an alibi. I'll give Eva a call when we get back to my house."

While River drove across town, conflicting thoughts tumbled through Lydia's head as she considered the revelation about the hat from every angle. Maybe it was just a generic white hat that Miles had seen? The man who had attacked her was strong. Norm was in decent shape, but he was in his late sixties. She couldn't get past what good grandparents Norm and Sheryl were. The more she thought about it, the less it seemed like a possibility. She just couldn't imagine them wanting her dead.

River's voice broke through her racing thoughts. "We can swing by your house and pick up some clothes if you like."

She nodded. "Let's do that."

River pulled up to her house, which looked dark and silent. "I wonder if a gas leak is something you could make happen on purpose?" The accident occurred right after Norm had been in the house alone.

"The timing is suspicious. I agree." Trying to find Elsie had been so all-consuming, she hadn't even called the insurance company to get the ball rolling on repairs. "I imagine there will be some kind of inspection so we will know for sure."

She pushed opened the car door.

While she waited for him on the sidewalk, River let Frankie out of the car.

Frankie followed them up the walk and waited while Lydia unlocked the door. She stepped aside so River and Frankie could go in first. While River and his partner made sure no one was lurking in the house, she studied the damage to her kitchen. The stove, which had been blown away from the wall, was in pieces all over the kitchen floor. Part of the counter had been blackened by the blast and everywhere there were broken dishes. Other than a bad smell the rest of the house seemed undamaged.

River stepped into the living room. "All clear."

Lydia hurried into her bedroom, pulled a bag from underneath the bed and tossed some clothes into it. She could hear River in the next room talking to Eva about checking into Norm and Sheryl's alibi.

Lydia stepped into the hallway and stared at Elsie's

slightly ajar door. She hadn't looked into the room since the kidnapping. She pushed the door open. The room was done in Elsie's favorite colors, pink and green. Books about animals stood on her nightstand. Even though her marriage had already been in turmoil, the day Elsie was born had been the happiest of her life.

Come back to me, baby girl.

River stood on the threshold of the bedroom. "Do you need a minute more?"

She appreciated his consideration. "No, thank you, I'm good." She grabbed Elsie's favorite stuffed animal, a bear named Mr. Binkins, and a book she loved, placing them in the bag and zipping it up. She had to think positive. When, not if, they found Elsie, she would be afraid, and familiar things would be a comfort.

River reached his hand out to carry the bag for her. Once they were in the patrol car, he headed back toward his place. "I looked at where the explosion happened. Some of the wires were stripped. I'm not an expert, but that might have caused a spark that ignited the gas when it was turned on."

A knot formed in her stomach. "Norm makes his living as a general contractor. I'm sure he knows something about that sort of thing."

They had only gone a few blocks and made one turn when he slowed down.

"Something wrong?"

"I think we're being followed. Don't look behind you."

Her heart beat a little faster. They were on a busy street with lots of box stores that had large parking lots. "Is it the tan SUV?"

"No. A white car, lower to the ground."

Norm and Sheryl owned a dark gray newer SUV and a

red compact car, but they could have borrowed a car from somewhere.

"I'm not going directly back to my house. Just in case. I don't want to lead them right to the place that so far has been safe for you."

She wondered if someone had been parked by her house and watching to see if she came back.

River did several quick turns then pulled into a furniture store parking lot that was filled with cars.

He turned the car engine off. "Let's just wait here for a few minutes."

She craned her neck. "Did the white car pull in, too?"

"The lot's too full to tell. But he stayed with us at least through the first quick turn." He tapped the steering wheel.

"I heard you talking to Eva about Sheryl and Norm's alibi. What's she going to look into if she doesn't just ask Debbie if they were at her house in Grand Junction?"

"DMV records will give the make and model of their cars. There might be cameras close to their house that show when they left and came back. She can get footage close to Debbie's house, too. Eva knows how to work things from all kinds of angles. We'll be able to break or confirm their alibi, and that's the first step."

"At least if Elsie is with them, I know she's safe." Small consolation.

River continued to check his mirrors. His voice softened. "Yes, that's one good thing."

The thought that hovered around the corners of her mind came front and center. Even if Norm and Sheryl thought they could do a better job raising Elsie, they wouldn't try to kill her. It seemed like she would have known if the man who had attacked her was Norm. The more she thought about it, the less likely it seemed that Sloane's parents, even if he had put pressure on them, would go that far.

She rested her head against the back of the seat and let out a heavy sigh. "All we talk about is things connected to finding Elsie."

"Yeah, it's hard to think about anything else. You know."

"Agreed." They'd been together almost nonstop since Elsie's disappearance, and she knew very little about River. "What made you decide to become a police officer?"

"It wasn't my first dream. I wanted to help people. Thought I would become a doctor and do cancer research." He shrugged and ran his hand through his blond hair. "I washed out of med school and I had to rethink my whole life."

"From doctor to police officer. That's a leap."

"I was with the volunteer search and rescue back then. I realized I felt way more like I was helping people doing that than memorizing anatomy. I liked working with the dogs. I liked being outside. When I got accepted at the police academy, I knew I wanted to be a K-9 officer."

"I guess sometimes you have to rethink your life," she said.

"For sure. What made you want to be a preschool teacher?"

"I always loved children. I didn't have any siblings growing up and I've always dreamed of having lots of children of my own. Teaching little kids was just a natural outlet."

His voice filled with compassion. "Sorry you didn't get that big family you hoped for."

It was River's kindness that she was drawn to.

"Guess I had to rethink my life when I realized staying with Sloane was too dangerous for both of us." Her throat grew tight and her voice cracked. "I'm just glad God gave me Elsie."

Leaning toward her, he rested his gaze on her for a long moment. "You've been through a lot. This is more than anyone should have to endure." He reached over and pulled a strand of her red hair behind her ear.

His expression and the warmth in his blue eyes were magnetic. She leaned toward him. Her heart fluttered as her cheeks flushed. She turned sideways and stared out the windshield. What was she doing? A second longer looking into those blue eyes and they would have kissed. Clearing her throat, she tugged on the front of her shirt. "How long do you suppose we'll have to sit here?"

He checked his mirrors again. "Guess it's okay to leave."

His phone rang. "Eva." He pressed the connect button. "You should hear this if it has to do with what she found about Sheryl and Norm's alibi." He placed the phone on the console. "Hey, Eva. Lydia's here with me. You got something for us?"

Lydia liked that River saw them as working together to find her daughter. Being sidelined and confined to a house was the most helpless feeling in the world.

Eva's crisp voice came through the line. "Just a little info, but I wanted to give it to you anyway. I haven't had much time to devote to this. I'm still doing a deep dive on trying to infiltrate these dark web adoption places. It's a bit of a challenge."

"But you found something related to Elsie's case?"

"Yes. I have a law enforcement friend in Grand Junction, so I was able to speed things up on that end. He was able to grab the CC footage close to the exit the grandparents would have used to get to the daughter's house directly the day they said they went there. No car matching either one of the two they own went by that camera on Sunday. It could be that they took a different exit. For whatever reason, they wanted to take the scenic route."

Lydia massaged the back of her neck where her muscles had tensed. Not the smoking gun that broke their alibi, but it didn't look good.

"Thanks for checking that out," said River.

"Anyway, when I get another free moment, I'll work their alibi from a different angle."

"Thanks, Eva. Maybe there's a way we can figure out when and if they ever left Ridge."

"That would be good, if you could be feet on the ground. I'll give it as much time as I can. We've got two missing girls we need to bring home. Take care, River, and you, too, Lydia," said Eva.

"Thank you." A lump had formed in Lydia's throat.

He started the engine and pulled out of the parking space, still looking around. "I'm not totally comfortable heading to the house just yet. Far as we know, my place is still safe for you, but we might be followed again."

Always in the back of her mind, Lydia heard a ticking clock where Elsie was concerned. She knew the same was true for Mia. Eva was probably working extreme overtime already. Just driving around or even being confined at River's house made her feel like she wasn't doing enough.

"You know, Norm and Sheryl live about five miles outside of Ridge. Why don't we just go by and talk to them and settle this once and for all?" Everything her in-laws had done since Elsie's disappearance showed they were supportive grandparents. "You said to Eva that we should work to break their alibi from here in town. I can just say I wanted to talk to them in person about Elsie, and we can get around to asking about their visit with Debbie. You can probably tell when someone is lying." Had Norm's visit and the phone calls all been a way of cementing the ruse that they cared about her well-being? It just didn't seem possible.

River's jaw hardened. It was clear he didn't like the idea.

She didn't like just sitting on her hands while her daughter was still missing. What if they were totally off base about Norm and Sheryl? All this work could be wasted time they could have spent finding who had really kidnapped her little girl.

"They won't try anything if you and Frankie are with me." She took in a sharp breath. "Maybe they have Elsie there."

River didn't answer right away. He cranked the steering wheel and drove through the parking lot. He didn't talk until he'd pulled out onto the street. "We're not going there alone. Let me find out if someone from the task force is close."

He must have felt as desperate as she did.

He parked the car and picked up his phone. It took only two phone calls before he got a positive response. Eli Blackwood was close by and could provide backup. River explained to Eli, "I'll text you the address. I'll have Lydia with me. The place is a short ways out of town."

After Lydia recited the address, River followed the directions his GPS gave him.

Lydia spoke up when they were about to turn into the subdivision where her in-laws lived. "We're about three minutes from where their house is."

"Good. We'll wait for Eli to get here. Wrangler is trained in suspect apprehension and protection. I hope we don't have to utilize that training."

Her stomach tied into knots. "Me, too."

Once Eli pulled up behind them in his patrol car, they

headed the short distance to her in-laws' house. Lydia tensed as the house she'd been to hundreds of times before came into view.

River wasn't so sure about this plan. Yes, they needed to follow every lead and having Lydia along, under the ruse of updating Norm and Sheryl, would mean that they wouldn't know that they were possible suspects. But what if the plan put Lydia in danger?

The houses in the subdivision were large, each situated on what looked to be lots that were at least half an acre. He could see a golf course in the distance. Norm and Sheryl must be pretty well off.

"There." Lydia pointed to a brown-and-white house that looked way too big for two people. Rosebushes bordered the edge of the yard. There were no cars in the driveway, and the house looked dark.

"It doesn't look like they're home unless their cars are in the garage." She pushed open the car door. "I'm going to knock on the door anyway."

"I assume Elsie comes here quite a bit?" If the dogs alerted to her scent, it would not be a surprise.

"We try to have a Sunday dinner every week. They canceled last Sunday because they were headed out to Debbie's. Or at least that's what they told me."

Elsie had been taken on a Monday.

Eli parked behind River. Both officers deployed their dogs.

"Why don't I check out the back of the house?" said Eli.

With Frankie by his side, River walked with Lydia to the front door. In light of all the attacks on Lydia, he found himself on high alert.

She rang the bell several times. The window by the door revealed no activity.

The triple garage had a window. He wandered over and peered inside. Only one car. The red compact.

An older man walking his poodle went by on the road. "Lydia?"

Lydia turned and walked toward him. "Pete?"

River moved in so he could hear the conversation.

"I'm so sorry about Elsie. I saw the story on the news."

So, the neighbor hadn't heard the story directly from the in-laws.

"Yes, I came by to update Sheryl and Norm," said Lydia.

"I haven't seen them since it happened." The man's gaze went from River to Eli, who had just come around the corner of the house with his K-9. He probably wondered why she needed such a strong police presence to keep her in-laws in the loop. River picked up on a degree of coldness from Pete toward Lydia. The neighbor had probably only heard the former in-laws' side of the story as to why she'd divorced their son.

"Are the police any closer to finding Elsie?"

River took a step nearer to Lydia. Pete studied him and Frankie for a long moment.

Lydia didn't skip a beat in giving a believable answer. "They're following some different leads. I just thought I should see Norm and Sheryl in person to talk to them about all that the police have been doing to find her."

Pete shifted his weight as the poodle did a half circle around him. "I don't think they've been home much. I might have seen their gray car pull up once. I just assumed they were visiting their daughter in Grand Junction. Her little guy has had some problems since he was born."

With the neighbors watching, it didn't seem like Norm

and Sheryl would bring Elsie back here if they were the ones who had her. Everything so far was circumstantial at best.

"Hope you find her soon." Pete said his goodbye and continued on down the road.

Lydia placed her hands on her hips and stared up the street. "Pete's house is right next door, and he's outside a lot, working in his yard."

"So his report that he only saw them once is probably accurate," said River.

"Like Pete said, maybe they're visiting Debbie again."

"It would be easy enough to get the Grand Junction police to put eyes on her house for a twenty-four-hour period to see if they show up or if their vehicle is parked there already. What we do know is they haven't been home."

"Why don't I just call them, saying I want to give them an update. I can work in asking them where they are. If they say they're at their home, we'll know they're lying."

It was clear that Lydia was having a hard time believing that Elsie's grandparents could be involved in something like this. "Okay, give them a call."

Lydia pulled her phone out and pressed buttons. Her face drained of color as it rang several times and then went to voice mail. She disconnected without leaving a message.

Eli stepped toward them. "Nothing in the backyard. No surprise that the girl's scent is all over the place. There's a bunch of trees back there, but Wrangler didn't pick up on any trail leading away from the property."

"Thanks, Eli."

They got into their respective patrol vehicles. As they pulled away, the quiet, dark house was disconcerting.

"I guess I'll just go back to your house and wait." Lydia sounded deflated.

"At least we have food to eat now." He tried to sound upbeat.

She laughed. "Really, River, it's not that hard to swing by a grocery store and grab a few things now and then."

He was glad his comment had elevated her mood. Anything to get her mind off the heaviness of what she was going through.

"I just get busy, and it's easier to go through a drive-through or grab a pizza."

"You need a wife. She would take care of that for you."

"Yeah, you think so." The joviality of the conversation seemed to have shifted. Why was she thinking about him being married? As much as he liked Lydia, he didn't even want to entertain the thought. His focus needed to be on finding Elsie.

When he pulled onto the road that led back to town, he paid more attention to the cars around him.

"Isn't there something else we could do here in town to confirm their alibi?"

River thought for a moment. They had to do something to either eliminate Sheryl and Norm as suspects or to home in on them. Once they had probable cause, they could secure warrants to examine credit card use and search the house and any other place they might have kept Elsie. "Why don't we grab a bite to eat at home and figure it out from there?"

Still looking for any suspicious vehicles, River pulled up in front of his house. After letting Lydia in and making sure it was safe, he took Frankie for a patrol around the outside of the house. The back of his house connected with a park where children played on the swings and a slide.

As he watched the children play, a sense of despair invaded his mind. This felt like Noah all over again. Maybe they should have looked at the grandparents sooner. Had he made the right choices, asked the right questions, understood the dynamics of the relationships of the people connected to Elsie?

It was clear Lydia couldn't see Norm and Sheryl as being involved with something as bad as this. Maybe she was right. Then where else could they look?

Frankie whimpered, pulling him out of his tangled thoughts. "Let's go get something to eat, huh?"

As he stepped inside, the image of Elsie from Lydia's phone was burned into his mind. He had to find her alive.

TWELVE

As she gathered the ingredients for the ham and Swiss sandwiches, Lydia wondered why she'd made the remark about River needing a wife. Was she picturing herself in that role? She shook her head at the idea. She was coming to rely on him, and he had been so kind and attentive, but she had to remind herself that he was just doing his job.

River came back in the house with Frankie.

"Lunch will be just a few minutes." It was well after two and her stomach was growling.

River sat down with his phone. "I have to text some of the task force and find out if any progress has been made finding the free clinic Gayle Gorman may have gone to in Denver."

She nodded, assembling the sandwiches, then toasting them and cutting up some fruit. They sat at the table and River said grace.

After he ate, River stayed busy on his phone and computer.

She found a book to distract her on River's bookshelf. She kept reading the same sentence over and over. There must be something more she could do to find Elsie. She rose from her chair and paced through the house. When she returned to the living room, River looked up from his laptop.

"If your in-laws have not been at their house or in Grand Junction, where else would they go?"

"Did you talk to the police in Grand Junction?"

"They did a drive-by. There's no sign of their other car there."

She'd just heard him talking to another task force member, but it was clear his mind was on Elsie as well.

"Not sure. They don't own like a cabin or a vacation home or anything. When they retired, they wanted to use their money and time to travel to foreign countries. They might even own a condo or time-share in one of them. They certainly have the money for that."

"Maybe they left the country. I can check with the airport to see if they flew out. Elsie's old enough that they would have had to buy a seat for her, too."

Lydia collapsed in a chair as tension invaded her chest. Was Elsie already in a different country? If Sloane had put them up to this, was he intending to join them later? It just seemed so far-fetched. She wondered if she should just call Sloane. She of all people would be able to tell if he was hiding something.

While River made a phone call to the Denver airport, she wandered back into the bedroom she was sleeping in. The stuffed animal she'd grabbed for Elsie, a brown bear, was peeking out of her bag. Its blue-button eyes stared at her blankly. She picked it up and held it to her chest.

She thought about what River had said about working a case from all angles. If Norm and Sheryl had been involved, they or their car would have been spotted heading to Ridge Mountain the day Elsie disappeared. If they'd been close to the trail, they couldn't have been in Grand Junction. Their alibi would be broken.

She let out a heavy breath.

None of this mattered if they'd already left the country with Elsie.

When she stepped back out into the living room, River was working on his laptop again. He looked up at her. "No one under the name of Norm and Sheryl Caldwell got on a plane with a three-year-old passenger. It would take time to put together fake ID that would fool TSA."

"I suppose that's good news." They could take a bus or drive their car. "I was thinking maybe we could go back out to the road that leads to Ridge Mountain. Maybe someone saw them or their car or a camera picked something up. That would mean they lied about being in Grand Junction."

"A gray SUV is kind of generic. Eva could track down the license number. If a camera picked that detail up, we'd know for sure."

"They had some distinctive bumper stickers, too. I would recognize them if I saw them. One was for a drone flying club that Norm is a member of and the other is for Estes Park."

"There're two different gas stations on the way up there. Let me finish what I'm doing here, and we can do that. Do you have a photo of Norm and Sheryl?"

"Yes, on my phone," she said. "I think I might lay down and rest while you finish up." She scrolled through her phone to find a photo of Sheryl and Norm. There were several, all of them with Elsie. Sadness and an ache like she'd never known washed through her when she saw Elsie's bright face and infectious smile.

She pulled up Norm's number. Her finger hovered over the connect button. They probably wouldn't pick up, just like before. They must have seen that she had called by now. And yet they hadn't called back, a sharp contrast to their initial show of concern for her.

She rested. When she opened her eyes, the sky was gray. It must be past dinnertime. They'd eaten such a late lunch, she wouldn't be hungry until dark. She rose and stepped into the living room. Both River and Frankie were gone. He wouldn't leave her here alone.

She peered out each of the living room windows and then moved to the kitchen that looked out on the back of the house. River stood watching the empty park while Frankie did her business. Just seeing him made her feel safe.

River came back inside, "Do you feel ready to go check out those gas stations."

"Sure." She grabbed her purse and they headed out the door to his patrol car. The sun was low on the horizon by the time they got on the mountain road that led up to the hiking trails.

The first gas station didn't have cameras. The clerk they questioned had been working that Monday but didn't remember an older couple with a woman in a white hat. Lydia showed her the picture on her phone.

"They would have been driving a gray SUV," said River.

The clerk, a stout woman with salt-and-pepper hair and glasses she kept on a chain, shook her head. "Monday's not a super-busy day on the trail, but I don't remember anyone like that."

By the time River drove to the last gas station before the hiking trail, the sky had grown even darker. The convenience store was nestled close to a forest. There were two other cars in the parking lot. River left Frankie in the patrol car but let her out of the kennel so she could move around more. They walked side by side toward the store entrance. Inside, a young man with a nose ring and yellow-tipped hair, stood behind the counter. His tie-dye T-shirt said Jesus Loves You.

"How can I help you folks?" He had a radiant smile.

River pulled out his badge. "I'm with the Ridge PD. We're investigating the disappearance of a little girl."

"Yeah, I saw that on the news." His gaze rested on Lydia. "I've been praying she'd be found."

His words touched Lydia. There were probably dozens of strangers praying for her little girl.

"I noticed you've got a camera on the gas pumps outside. Do you keep that footage?"

"Just for a week and then we record over it. I can get the recording for Monday and set you up in the break room to watch it."

"That would be good," said River.

After the clerk helped another customer who had come in, he dug through the stack of DVDs and put one in the player.

They both pulled up a chair. "Get ready for some riveting television watching," said River.

River's sense of humor even in the most trying moments eased her anxiety. "I'm on pins and needles."

River fast-forwarded through the tape. "We'll start about two hours before the time of the abduction."

"It was an afternoon hike, so that would have been about eleven." Norm and Sheryl had known about the hike. She kept them informed about all Elsie's school activities, many of which they came to. Her stomach twisted into a knot. How could they have been plotting something like this while they'd sat through Elsie's school play and attended grandparents' day? It just didn't seem possible.

Lydia watched the video as one car after another got gas; some people entered the store as well. "Do they have tapes for the interior of the store?"

"I'm sure they do, but let's start here. This camera picks up the pumps, most of the parking lot, and you can see when someone walks toward the store entrance. If it comes to that, Eva can get copies of the recordings. She has software that will look for people matching Norm and Sheryl's description. The white hat would be the most obvious thing to keyword in. Way faster than going through manually."

After about twenty minutes, Lydia stood. "I have to go to the bathroom. I'll be right back."

Leaving her purse behind, she stepped out into the main room where the clerk was looking at his phone. No one else was in the store. He looked up.

"Your restrooms?"

He grabbed a key off the wall. "You have to go outside and to the left."

She stepped outside into the twilight of early evening. There were no other cars in the parking lot besides the patrol vehicle. She could see Frankie's head in the front seat as she sat behind the steering wheel.

Lydia stuck the key in the lock and turned it. A noise in the trees at the back side of the convenience store drew her attention. A man wearing gloves and a mask reached out and grabbed her. A needle went into her arm. There was no time to scream before his hand went over her mouth, and she was dragged into the forest. She could feel herself slipping away. Her eyelids were heavy, and her limbs felt like they'd had weights placed on them.

The last thing she heard was Frankie's barking.

River stared at the screen while holding the remote. Even on fast forward, watching the comings and goings at the gas pumps was tedious. As busy as Eva was, maybe sending the files to her would be faster.

The store clerk poked his head into the storage room. "Your dog is going ballistic out there."

"What?" He set the remote down on a box and jumped up from his chair. By the time he got outside, his heart was pounding. Frankie never sounded the alarm over nothing. He hurried around the side of the building to where the restrooms were. He walked toward the one for women, lifting his fist to knock on the door when he saw the key stuck in the lock.

All the air left his lungs as he wheezed in a breath and turned a half circle.

Something had happened to Lydia. He looked toward the forest at the rear of the store and then out at the parking lot. His patrol car was the only vehicle in the lot. He sprinted toward it. It had been less than five minutes since she'd left the store. Frankie might be able to track her.

His hand was on the driver's-side door, where Frankie moved from one seat to the other, clearly agitated. He caught movement in his peripheral vision and turned to see the tan SUV emerge from the trees and pull out onto the main road.

He yanked the door open and jumped in behind the wheel just as the SUV disappeared over the hill. Frankie settled into the passenger seat.

"Hold on, girl." He pulled out of the parking lot and floored it. There were no other cars on the road at this hour. He could see the red glow of the other vehicle's taillights. The SUV abruptly turned and disappeared into the trees.

He sped up, turning onto the dirt road where the SUV had gone. The canopy of tall evergreens made the early evening even darker. He switched on his lights. His car bumped along. Years of rainfall without repairs had made the road rutty. He didn't see the other vehicle anywhere. He had to be on this road, there had been no other turnoffs.

"We've got to find her." He was having a hard time taking a deep breath. Frankie licked his face. If it hadn't been for her, the abductor would have been long gone by the time River wondered why Lydia hadn't returned from the restroom.

He kept his eyes on the road but reached out to rub Frankie's head. "You're about the best partner a guy could have."

The trees thinned out and turned into rolling hills. He spotted the other vehicle's taillights. The tan SUV turned at what must be a crossroad at least a quarter mile away.

He pressed the gas, but progress was slow on the primitive road. He came to the crossroad and turned in the direction he'd seen the other SUV go. The driver must have gone over the hill.

River prayed that he would get to Lydia in time.

When he got to the top of the hill, he saw a forest down below but no vehicle.

He drove to the edge of the forest as the muscles at the back of his neck twisted. Still no sign of the SUV.

His gaze bounced around the landscape. Had the driver turned off his headlights so he'd be harder to spot at a distance? From the top of the hill, he could see several intersecting roads. Could the SUV have pulled into the trees? Maybe there was even a road there that River couldn't see from his vantage point. There were too many places the guy could have gone.

Frankie whimpered.

"We're not giving up," said River. "We just need some help." He grabbed his radio.

The police dispatcher's voice came over the line. "Officer Jameson, what is it?"

A lump had formed in his throat. "Galvanize search and rescue and get as many officers as you can over by Ridge Mountain." If any of the task force members were close to Ridge, he knew they would come and help as well.

"Location?"

"The dirt road on the east side of the forest after the last gas station. I'm about four miles in."

"What is the situation?"

"A woman has been kidnapped in a tan SUV." He closed his eyes, feeling a tightening through his chest. "Her name is Lydia Caldwell. We have to find her before it's too late."

THIRTEEN

The first thing Lydia was aware of was the rocking motion of the SUV from the back seat where she lay. Her brain felt like it had been stuffed full of cotton balls. Her muscles were mush. Whatever she'd been injected with had knocked her out.

Her abductor must have been in a hurry. He'd not taken the time to tie her up. When she tried to sit up, it felt like a weight was attached to the back of her head.

She could see the man from the back, still wearing the mask that hid his face..

She couldn't tell much about him. Was it Norm? She couldn't be sure.

The SUV kept rolling over the hills. Stars twinkled in the dark night sky. He must be taking her some place remote to kill her. That had been the plan all along. Fear made it hard to take in a deep breath. She turned on her side, feeling around on the floor of the back seat and under the seat. She needed some kind of weapon for when he stopped. Her hands touched something metal. A wrench.

The vehicle slowed down. Hiding the wrench underneath her body, she flipped over onto her stomach. The attacker must have thought that whatever he'd knocked her out with would last until he reached his destination. Playing along with his assumption would give her the element of surprise.

The SUV stopped.

The back door opened. She lay still, feigning unconsciousness. The wrench felt cold in her hand.

He pulled on her feet then flipped her over so that she was on her side and halfway out of the vehicle.

She sat up, smashing the wrench against his bent head three times. He stumbled backward. Clutching the wrench, she jumped out of the SUV. Her muscles were still weak. She could hear the sound of rushing water in the distance and see an evergreen forest off to the side.

The rumbling hum of the river grew louder as she ran. The man reached out and grabbed the back of her shirt. Angling sideways, she hit the man in the shoulder twice. He groaned in pain and let go of her. She sprinted through the darkness over rocks. The river was close.

The man came after her again, tackling her and knocking her to the ground. She dropped the wrench. Landing on her stomach, she tried to crawl away. He held on to her ankle. She picked up a rock, bent her body and threw it. It hit his shoulder. The distraction gave her time to scramble to her feet.

Gaining strength, she ran, still unable to see where she was going.

He grabbed her from behind. She swung around to free herself but stepped too close to the edge of the steep bank. Lydia fell through the air and splashed into the cold water of the river. She could see the man above her making his way down the steep incline. The water pulled her under as the current carried her to the center of the river. She gulped for air when the force of the river pushed her upward.

The attacker followed along the river's edge.

She tried to swim toward the opposite bank. When the water grew shallower, she was finally able to stand up. Weighted by the water, her clothes dragged her down as she made her way to the shore.

When she looked over her shoulder, the dark figure was still pacing along the opposite bank.

Shivering, she dragged herself to her feet. She did not know who the attacker was, but she knew now, after being so close to him for so long, that it wasn't Norm.

She bent over as she walked, trying to catch her breath. The cold had seeped into her skin. The man had retreated to the SUV, but she didn't see headlights go on. He wasn't leaving. The bang of a rifle shot caused her to fall on her belly. He'd gotten his gun and was shooting at her from across the river.

She lay still, hoping the darkness would shield her. Another bullet hit a rock in front of her. The shot was close enough that it caused her whole body to jerk. She crawled away from the riverbank. Two more shots were fired before she reached the brush that provided some cover. When she peered over her shoulder, the SUV was no longer parked on the riverbank. She feared that there was a bridge he could cross to come after her again. Despite muscle fatigue and cold, she broke into a jog.

Lydia kept heading away from the river, stumbling through the dark. She had no idea where she was. She'd left her phone in her purse. How far had her abductor driven off the main road? Miles? She kept moving, searching for any sign of civilization, lights, a cabin, a camper.

The shivering intensified. She wrapped her arms over her chest as water dripped from her wet clothes.

Cold and bent over, she trudged forward. She may have escaped the attacker in the short term, but she was far from safe.

* * *

Fear sank into River's chest like a knife when he heard the rifle shots far off in the distance. With Frankie in the lead, he ran toward where the sound had come from. Two other dogs and their handlers who were searching the same area came up behind him but remained spread out.

To keep up with Frankie, he burst into a sprint.

He could hear a river in the distance. The closer they got to the river, the faster Frankie and the other dogs moved. The hound behind him was baying, cutting through the silence of the night. Off to the side, a chopper flew overhead.

They arrived at the river. The intensity with which the K-9s rallied signaled that Lydia had come this way. Frankie and the other dogs lead the handlers down a steep incline to the river's edge. All the K-9s moved back and forth along the shore. The hound dove in until he was called back by his handler.

Task force member Maren Anderson came and stood by River with her Doberman, Haven.

"Do you think she went into the river?"

"It looks that way." River pulled the walkie-talkie off his belt that he'd gotten from the search and rescue team. He knew the pilot of the chopper by name. "Ansel, can you touch down over by the river? I need to get across."

"Can do," said Ansel. "I think I see you on the ground there." The chopper banked and then drew closer to them, its beating blades growing louder.

Even though they were spread out, none of the searchers or police officers had spotted the tan SUV. The glint of something shiny on the rocks caught River's eye. He bent over and picked up a spent rifle shell. He saw another not too far from the first.

The shell could have been there from a long time ago,

but he'd heard those shots. He stared off into the dark flowing water. Fear gripped his heart. Had she been shot and fallen into the river?

The idea made his breath catch. He couldn't imagine a world without her. The chopper touched down, and he and Frankie got in. Another nose and set of eyes would be nice, but there was no room in the chopper for another K-9 and handler.

The chopper lifted off.

River spoke above the mechanical hum of the engine. "Stay close to the river for a bit. Then we'll search farther away on the land."

The pilot nodded.

The searchlights illuminated the dark flowing water below. When the pilot dropped elevation, River could see details on the trees and brush growing close to the river. He feared he would see Lydia's body being pulled by the current or lying face down on the shore.

After they'd gone a sufficient distance without seeing anything, the pilot turned back around.

River continued to search while Ansel flew in a serpentine pattern, getting farther and farther away from the river. A white spot on the ground caught River's attention.

"There." Lydia had been wearing a white shirt. Her jacket and yoga pants were a darker color.

"I see it." The chopper dropped down even more and moved toward the light-colored object. It was a shirt draped over a bush.

"Let Frankie and me out."

"Give me a second here," said Ansel. "I need to find a flat area to touch down."

While he waited for the pilot to find a safe landing spot, River felt like an anaconda was wrapping itself around his chest, crushing all the air out of his lungs. Lydia had to be down there. She had to be alive. Yet if she was around here, she must've heard the helicopter. Why hadn't she come to an open area and waved her arms?

The chopper landed. River and Frankie jumped out. Frankie took the lead as they moved in the direction River had seen the white shirt. Everything looked different once he was on the ground. Frankie seemed to know where she was going. He'd trust her nose over his eyes. They entered a patch of brush. It took some circling around to find the white shirt. It was still wet, and it looked like the one she'd been wearing. She'd put the shirt out as a signal.

River shouted Lydia's name as Frankie dashed ahead of him, disappearing into the brush. Frankie's intense barking filled the air. Pushing through the thick brush, River ran toward the sound. He came to an open area. Frankie paced around Lydia, who lay on her side, not moving.

He let out the breath he'd been holding. They'd found her.

River dropped to the ground. Her skin was cold to the touch, but she had a pulse. She was alive.

She said something so quietly, he couldn't understand it. He leaned closer to her mouth.

"You came for me," she whispered.

He brushed a strand of wet hair out of her eyes. "'Course I did." He pulled his walkie-talkie to speak to the pilot. "I found her. She's in late-stage hypothermia. We need to get her to a medical facility ASAP."

"I can't move in any closer."

"We'll come to you." He secured the walkie-talkie on his belt and leaned to help Lydia to her feet. Once she was standing, her knees buckled. He lifted her into his arms and carried her.

Her head rested again his chest.

She spoke in a soft voice. "I think I love you."

River blinked. Where was that sentiment coming from? People with advanced hypothermia often hallucinated. He wondered if that was what was going on.

When they stepped through the brush, he could see the pilot running toward them, holding a litter. He laid Lydia in it and the two men carried her to the chopper, securing her in the back seat and covering her with a blanket. River sat in the copilot seat with Frankie squeezed in at his feet.

As the chopper took off, he craned his neck to look at Lydia. Pale and motionless, she looked more like a porcelain doll than a person. Lydia had been coherent enough to recognize him. She'd had the presence of mind to put out the shirt as a signal before putting her jacket back on and collapsing.

The helicopter ride seemed to take forever as they flew over treetops. A dirt road and then the paved road that led into Ridge came into view. The pilot radioed ahead to the hospital. When they touched down on the roof, a medical crew was waiting with a gurney.

They transferred Lydia's limp body and hurried over to the elevator doors that said Medical Staff Only. The pilot took off while River and Frankie made their way down the stairs.

He prayed that it was not too late for Lydia.

FOURTEEN

As medical staff hovered over her, checked her vitals and covered her with warm blankets, Lydia was only partially aware of what was going on. She felt herself drifting in and out. Something was said about her heart sounding stronger.

As she floated toward unconsciousness, the memory of being carried by River materialized in her mind, warming her even faster than the blanket that was laid on top of her. In her near comatose state, she'd said something to him. She didn't remember what. The vision of lying shivering on the cold hard ground and then looking up to see his face was the last image that popped into her head before she drifted off. She'd been praying for someone to rescue her.

River was an answer to a prayer.

When she opened her eyes, the curtains in the hospital room were drawn but early morning light snuck in between them.

A warm hand gripped hers.

River.

"Hey." Affection made his face glow.

She raised her head to see him more clearly. "Hey. I slept all night?"

"Yes, the doctors say you're out of the woods." He leaned

a little closer to her and squeezed her hand. "I was afraid you weren't going to make it. When I found you, you looked…"

"…like I was close to gone."

He nodded. "It scared me. You were still conscious. You said something kind of out there."

"What was that?"

"You said 'I love you.'"

Lydia's cheeks flushed with warmth. "Oh…my." So that's what she'd said when her defenses were down. Was it true?

River shifted in his chair. "It must have just been the hallucinating that happens during advanced hypothermia."

"Yes, that must have been it," she said. River seemed to want to dismiss the sentiment.

"You were just overjoyed that I showed up?"

"That must have been what was going on. Sure." There was a part of her that wondered if the hypothermia had loosened her inhibitions, and she'd spoken a truth that her conscious mind would never accept. She let go of his hand, the warmth of his touch fading slowly from her skin.

She stared at the ceiling, wishing the awkward moment would end.

River leaned toward her. "Did you see the man who attacked you?"

She sat up and brushed a strand of hair out of her eyes. "Not really, but I know it wasn't Norm. This man held me down. He was close to me. I was in the car with him for a long time. People have a smell, a presence. I don't know how to explain it."

Elsie's grandfather would not attack her in such a brutal way.

River shifted in his seat. "I can take you back to my place soon as the doctor's checked you out."

"Thank you."

"Frankie's waiting in the patrol car. I arranged for it to be brought over here."

"You stayed all night?"

"I made phone calls and took care of some stuff. The clerk at that gas station is going to send Eva a digitized file of that camera footage since we didn't get through it all."

"But the man who attacked me wasn't Norm."

"I know, but we need to be thorough. You said yourself—he still wore a mask."

River hadn't let go of the idea that her in-laws were somehow involved. The more she thought about it, the more absurd the idea seemed to her. She'd sat across a dinner table from them. They'd come to Elsie's christening and her birthday parties. Even though they did those things to have a relationship with Elsie, she couldn't imagine Norm attacking her in such a violent and close way.

River rose from his chair. "We can talk about it later. I'll see if I can have the doctors sign you out. I have another video call to do with the task force later today."

He left the room. A sense of emptiness invaded her mind. She didn't want to get in an argument with River about the investigation. They were both doing the best they could.

Within the hour, Lydia was dressed and ready to go.

They drove back to River's place. When they stepped inside, Lydia spotted Elsie's teddy bear on the couch where she'd left it. The weakness she felt from the hypothermia and seeing the toy caused the tears to flow. "Where is my little girl?"

She turned back to River, who gathered her into his arms while she cried. She tilted her head to gaze into his blue eyes. He bent close and his lips brushed over hers, a kiss as gentle as the brush of butterfly wings that lifted some of the sadness off her.

He stepped back, shaking his head. "Whoa. First you say you love me and now I go and kiss you. What is up with us?"

She detected fear in his voice. She felt it, too. After Sloane, she'd vowed to remain single. In her world, relationships meant the possibility of deep pain. Never again. "It's just everything that's happened. The doctors said I wouldn't feel like my old self for several days."

"Yes, that must be it. Lot of dramatic stuff for both of us." He hurried across the room, grabbed his laptop from the side table by the sofa and set it on the kitchen table.

She avoided making eye contact with River while he got ready for the video call. She rushed into the kitchen, not sure what she intended to do there. The kiss had her all discombobulated.

"Guess I'll make some coffee. You want some?"

"Sure," he said.

Doing something productive would get her mind off of how desperately she wanted to be back in River's arms again.

River stared at the black screen of his laptop. It was still another five minutes before the video call with the task force was set to start. When he'd been standing close to Lydia, the urge to kiss her again had been overwhelming.

Even now, he was keenly aware of her presence as she moved around the kitchen. She was a woman in crisis. He didn't want to take advantage when she was all over the place emotionally. Maybe if Elsie was back safe and this nightmare ended, he would have a clearer perspective on his feelings.

The truth was, when he'd thought she might die, he'd realized how much he cared about her.

She came over and set a cup of hot coffee down on the

table. Her shoulder brushed against his, causing his heart to flutter.

"Meeting hasn't started yet?"

He clicked keys, trying to look busy. "Just a few more minutes." The online meeting room, with only him signed in came up on the screen.

One by one, the other faces popped up on the screen starting with Emmett. Eva was the last to make an appearance after Eli, Lizzie and Maren.

"How is Lydia doing?" Eva asked.

"Yeah, we heard what happened," said Lizzie.

River glanced over his shoulder. Lydia must have retreated to the bedroom. He looked back at the screen. "She's on the road to recovery."

"That's good to hear, River," Emmett said. "I know everyone's time is valuable, so let's officially start the meeting. Thank you all for showing up. I know with Elsie's case and the investigation centered on Mia's disappearance, all of us have been putting in substantial overtime. There's been a slight shift in the focus of the baby snatching case. Lizzie, I know you and Autumn questioned staff at several homes in various towns for unwed mothers. Eli as well did some poking around in Denver."

"Nothing in our interviews set off alarm bells," said Eli.

Eva piped up. "If there had been any red flags, a whistle blower of any variety, I would have found a way to pull the financials on those places."

"Anyway, what we're starting to believe is that these young women are not being kept at one particular place." Emmett's head shifted slightly on the screen. "It would just be too easy for them to be caught. We believe that several locations are being used. Locations that probably aren't connected with medical facilities or pregnancy homes."

"So that means," said River, "that an OB doctor and probably a nurse with delivery experience must go to wherever these locations are when it's time for the baby to be born."

"Exactly," said Emmett. "We need to shift from locations to who might be involved in the delivery, maybe a doctor or nurse who lost his or her license."

"Or even someone with a lot of debt who needs to create income on the side and is willing to do it in a shady way," Maren added.

"I'm checking legal filings and news stories for any leads," said Eva.

"We still need to keep questioning staff at clinics, just alter your line of inquiry. As you interact with people at these places, find out if there are any former employees who may be disgruntled," said Emmett. "That might be a way to root out some suspects who would have motive beyond what Eva can do on her end."

"Got it," said Lizzie.

River shifted in his seat. Lydia had come back into the living room and sat down on the sofa to read a book. He found himself being extremely aware of her presence and her movements. It divided his attention from the meeting.

"River? You look like you were thinking about something."

"No, I just..." He glanced toward the sofa where Lydia sat out of view. "I was just wondering if we've located the clinic that Gayle went to in Denver."

"Still poking around," said Lizzie.

On the screen, Maren looked to the side and shook her head. "I just keep thinking about Mia out there somewhere afraid. She probably doesn't realize that once the baby is born, her life will be over."

A hushed silence fell between the members of the task

force. It felt like a weight lay on River's chest. Somewhere in Colorado, Mia Andrews was alone in a room, feeling her baby move around as she got closer to her due date in October. The image made him shiver. "We have to find her," he whispered.

The others nodded.

"I spoke to Dodger and his wife yesterday," said Emmett. "Just to give them an update. He and Clara are still praying and remaining hopeful, but I can tell you that this is tearing them up after losing their daughter and now their granddaughter is missing."

"Dodger has done so much to support K-9 programs. We have to do this for him. For Mia," said River.

Eli tugged on his beard and nodded. "And for the three other babies that have already been born."

"I just hope they were adopted by people who love them," said River.

"That's all for now. I'll be in touch with each of you individually if I have stronger directives," said Emmett. "River, how is the investigation into Elsie's disappearance going?"

He glanced over at Lydia, who put her book down and sat up straighter.

"We still don't have any strong leads as to who would do this. Or where the child might be. We're looking into the grandparents as a possibility. But Lydia doesn't think the man who abducted her was her father-in-law."

"I'm trying to help on that end," said Eva. "River, if you could stay on for a few minutes after the meeting adjourns, I have something to share with you."

"Sure," he said.

"Stay safe out there and let's be praying for Mia's return." Emmett leaned a little closer to the screen. "And for Elsie too."

* * *

One by one, the faces disappeared from the screen until it was just Eva.

"River, I know you want to resolve Elsie's disappearance. I'm trying to help as much as I can. The workload on Mia's case just keeps expanding."

"I feel bad that I can't help more with the footwork for that case. I'll be a hundred percent if can just get Elsie back safe in her mother's arms."

From the sofa where she sat, Lydia had turned toward him, listening to the conversation.

"Anyway, I did a quick scan of the digital file from that convenience store. There were several vehicles that came up as matches when I put in search parameters. The grandparents' car is kind of generic. I'm wondering if there is a way to identify it."

Lydia rose from the sofa and peered over River's shoulder. She was standing close enough that River could smell her floral perfume.

"Eva, thank you for doing this. Norm had some bumper stickers on the back of the car that I would recognize if I saw them," she said.

"I can send photos of the three cars that came up. I think I can isolate an image of the back of each car. It's taken from a distance, so it won't be the highest quality when I blow it up."

"One of the bumper stickers had distinctive neon colors," said Lydia. "Even if it was blurry, I would be able to recognize it."

"Okay. I'll send the images to River's phone. I got to get back to work. Lydia, we're all praying for Elsie's safe return."

"Thank you. I appreciate all that everyone has done."

"Take care. I'll get those to you as fast as I can." Eva waved goodbye and then disappeared from the screen.

Lydia sat in the chair kitty-corner from River. She stared off into the distance. "I guess we just wait now."

"I'm sure Eva will get it done as fast as she can."

"I don't think it's them. Fine, they think they could do a better job raising Elsie, but to kill me? That doesn't make any sense."

"Okay, so who else would want to kill you?"

"I don't know." Her eyes glazed with tears as she placed her hand on her mouth and shook her head. "I just don't know." She rose and ambled into the kitchen. "Do you want more coffee?" Her voice sounded brittle and tired.

He stared into his half-empty coffee cup. "I'm good."

She fussed around in the kitchen, poured herself a cup of coffee and sat back down in the living room.

As if he were flipping through index cards, River mentally reviewed everything they'd learned since Elsie had been kidnapped. The car that had been spotted on the dirt road had probably taken her away. Was she even now somewhere in the city? He was still baffled by the way that Frankie had lost the scent. As if Elsie had been taken up into the air. Frankie hadn't followed the scent out to the road where the car must have been parked, so maybe Elsie hadn't been taken away in that car. The evidence was confusing.

His phone dinged that he had a text. "It's Eva."

Lydia pushed up from her seat and came toward him.

He read the text.

I sent the files to your computer.

River tensed as he placed his fingers on the keyboard. "Let's have a look at those photos."

FIFTEEN

Lydia's stomach tightened as she sat down and scooted her chair closer to River's computer. He clicked on the first file. The car was a lighter gray than Norm's.

She shook her head.

He brought up the second image. Though not readable, two bumper stickers were visible. Lydia sat back in her chair as her heartbeat drummed in her ear. "That's their car." She rose and paced, wrapping her arms around herself. The numbness and the sensation that she was floating overtook her.

Her former in-laws had lied about where they'd been on the morning of Elsie's disappearance.

River rushed to her side and led her over to the couch. He sat beside her, close enough that their shoulders were touching.

Just having him close helped calm her churning emotions and racing thoughts.

Frankie rose where she'd been sleeping and trotted over to Lydia's side, nudging her hand.

Lydia's mind was spinning. Norm had come to her house to feign support for her, knowing that Elsie was with Sheryl. That's why he'd made up the story about Sheryl being too upset to visit. One of them needed to stay with Elsie. Her mother's distress had meant nothing to him. It had all been an act to make them look innocent. They were not the people she thought they were. She rested her hand against her forehead. "I still don't think Norm is the one who attacked me all those times."

"Could be that he hired someone." River let out a heavy breath. "We need to talk to Sloane and find out what he knows. If the rehab place still says he can't talk to people outside the facility, Emmett can see to it that we get a court order."

River was a man of action, and he was focused on the next step in the investigation. She simply could not absorb this new revelation.

Norm and Sheryl had most likely abducted their granddaughter. How could she not have seen who they really were? "I'm a fool. I believed Sloane's lies about the life we would have together. I trusted Norm and Sheryl. I wanted a family so bad." She rose from the sofa pacing and combing her fingers through her hair. She took in a sharp breath. "This is my fault. I'm a bad mother."

"No, that's not true." River wrapped his arms around her, making soothing sounds while he swayed and held her. He smoothed his hand over her hair.

He pulled away from the hug but rested his hands on her cheeks. "I'm calling the rehab place and getting Sloane on the phone. You can listen in, if you want to. He doesn't have to know that you're there. You know him. You'd be able to tell if he's lying."

Staring into his blue eyes quelled the tumultuous feelings. "At least I know that if Elsie's with them, she's not been harmed." The idea helped her take a deep breath as he stood and moved over to the table.

River sat down and pressed numbers on his phone. When

a woman answered, River identified himself as a police officer and explained the situation. "I know you said part of the protocol of the program was not to have contact with outside influences, but this is an emergency situation."

"Sloane is far enough in the program that he is allowed limited outside contact if he wants. I can ask him to speak to you, but he may choose not to," the woman responded. "The clients don't have access to television or the internet, so he doesn't know about his daughter. He's had no outside communication with anyone since he checked himself in. Give me a minute to explain the situation to him and then I'll call you back. Either he'll come on the line, or I'll let you know he refused."

"Okay," said River. River pressed buttons on his phone. "I'm sending this news to the task force group chat. If we can come up with a possible location for where Elsie might be, we're going to need all hands on deck. Some of them may be close to Ridge already."

After he sent the text to the task force, they both stared at the phone.

The anticipation made it hard for her to breathe. "Are you sure you don't want that cup of coffee?"

"I'll take it."

She poured the coffee for him and then sat down again. Her hand rested on the table. He reached over and covered her hand with his and looked directly into her eyes.

"Lydia, what you said about being a bad mother… I don't ever want to hear you say that again. You're a good mother."

She stared into his eyes for a long moment. "I want to believe that. I was a poor judge of character where Sloane was concerned, and now with Norm and Sheryl. I don't know that I would ever trust myself again, especially in a romantic situation."

River winced at her comment. She just didn't trust herself to fall in love again.

The phone rang. They both jumped.

The same woman's voice came across the line. "Sloane needed a minute to pull himself together. I have to tell you, he seemed genuinely shocked when I told him about Elsie. Oh, here he comes down the hallway."

A minute passed and then a man's bass voice came through the speaker. "You the cop that's looking for my little girl?"

"Yes, I'm Officer Jameson. It appears that your mother and father may have taken her. Do you know anything about this?"

"Mom and Dad are involved?" His surprise sounded genuine. "I didn't put them up to it, if that's what you're asking," said Sloane. "Look, I'm trying to turn over a new leaf. Being in this program has given me a lot of time to think."

"So, you didn't encourage them to take Elsie away from her mother?"

Sloane didn't answer right away. Lydia felt like she couldn't inhale a breath as they waited in the tense silence.

When Sloane spoke, it sounded like he was crying. "I was a very angry man when Lydia divorced me. I blamed her for everything. I probably said things to my parents that poisoned them against her. I'm so sorry I did that. In this program, they teach you that you have to own your choices. That's my part in what has happened to my little girl. She and Lydia deserve better than me. It was the best thing for Elsie that Lydia got sole custody."

Lydia's eyes glazed. The man she was hearing on the phone was not the same man who had driven drunk with their daughter. Though all the damage he'd done to her meant she felt no deep love for him, Lydia was glad it appeared he'd changed. The apology meant a great deal to her.

"Do you have any idea where they may have taken Elsie?"

"I can't think of any place. I will tell you that Dad can be kind of a bully. Mom just goes along with what he says to keep the peace. This program has made me see family dynamics more clearly."

"Are you sure you don't know where they are?"

"Honestly, I don't. I'm not trying to protect them."

Lydia leaned closer to River and whispered in his ear so Sloane wouldn't hear. "I believe him."

"Thank you for your time, Mr. Caldwell. If you do think of where they might be keeping the child, please get in touch with me."

"I will." Sloane gulped. "Officer Jameson, please find Elsie."

"We've got a bunch of officers on this. Everyone wants to bring Elsie home safe to her mother."

"That's the best place for her to be. I was never much of a father, but Lydia was a great mom."

A tear flowed down Lydia's cheek.

"Thank you, Mr. Caldwell." River clicked the disconnect button and sat back in his chair. "So where are they?"

Lydia shook her head. "Maybe they haven't left the state yet, but that must be their ultimate plan, to take Elsie to a foreign country. I still think that the man who attacked me at the river wasn't Norm. The other times it happened so quick, but that time I was in the car with him for a long time." Lydia just couldn't imagine him attacking her in such a direct way.

"They must be getting help from someone." River rubbed his chin. "So, that means we look at every known associate of both Sheryl and Norm and start questioning them."

"Do we have that kind of time? If they are still in the area, it's just a matter of time before they find a way to leave." Again, she felt as if a weight had been placed on her lungs.

Her breathing was shallow. "There has to be a faster way, River. Please."

River spoke in a calm voice. "I need you to think about who they associate with. Anyone who might be above the law."

"I have no idea. He's a retired contractor and she managed an office supply store. Honestly, my interaction with them was in relationship to Elsie. From the time I met them, they were always a little cold to me. I guess they thought I wasn't good enough for their son."

River let out a heavy breath. "Not true. You were too good." He paced into the kitchen. "You're right. Going through known associates is time-consuming, and it sounds like it would be a rabbit trail anyway. Maybe we should pray to come up with some leads."

"That's a good idea." She reached her hands toward him.

They held hands while River prayed. "God, we need Your help. We need to find Elsie before she's taken out of the country. Show us where to look, what leads we need to pursue, so we don't waste time."

Lydia opened her eyes. "Give me a minute. I'm going to go splash some water on my face and see if I can clear my head."

"Okay, I need to take Frankie outside," said River.

Lydia retreated to her bathroom. The cold water felt good on her face. She reached for a towel. It bothered her that she had not seen through Norm and Sheryl's act in the early hours of the kidnapping. Norm had come to see her. Even before that, Sheryl had called, acting concerned.

She gasped.

The phone call.

Lydia ran back into the living room and then outside, where River was walking the perimeter of the park with

Frankie. As she rushed across the yard, she glanced side to side, keenly aware that she was exposed. So far, it appeared that her attacker had not figured out she was staying here.

She sprinted toward him. "Sheryl called me on her cell the morning after Elsie had been taken. There must be a way to trace where that phone call came from. That has to be where they're keeping Elsie."

It took River only a second to realize that this might be the breakthrough they'd prayed for. River ran back to his house with Frankie and Lydia. Once inside, Lydia grabbed her phone and recited Sheryl phone number while River contacted Eva.

"Hello?"

"Eva, I know you have a lot on your plate, but if you could do something for me right now, we might be able to find Elsie."

"Sure, what is it?"

"I need to know if you can find out where a phone call was made from."

"Easy-peasy," said Eva. "It's just a matter of figuring out what towers the call pinged off of."

River recited the number. "It was the morning after Elsie was taken."

"Give me just a little bit of time. I'll get back to you as fast as I can."

River hung up. From where they stood in the living room, Lydia gazed at him and then fell into his arms. "I hope this works."

"Me, too," said River.

The screech of tires outside on the street reached his ears a second before the front window shattered. He got a glimpse of the tan SUV racing by. His hand went over

Lydia's back as he pulled her to the ground. Another shot was fired.

"They found us."

More shots came through the back window. There were two shooters.

"Get to the garage. Get in the car. Take Frankie."

Lydia crawled on all fours as more shots were fired through the back and front windows.

River reached up to grab his gun and his keys. He still had his phone in his hand. He dialed the Ridge Police Department as he made his way toward the open door that led to the garage. "This is Officer Jameson. I'm being shot at in my home."

A quick glance out the front window revealed that the tan SUV was not parked outside, but that didn't mean it wouldn't be coming back for another drive-by.

He heard the window in Lydia's bedroom shatter. One of the shooters must have moved in even closer. He hurried into the garage and got behind the wheel of his patrol vehicle. Lydia held the garage door remote.

"Tell me when to open it."

Frankie was in the back seat in her kennel. With his heart pounding, River fixed his gaze on the rearview mirror. "Now." After starting the engine, he shifted into Reverse.

The garage door rose. The street looked clear. He floored it and made a tight turn, shifting into Drive.

"He's coming back up the street." Fear permeated Lydia's words.

River sped up the street. In the distance, he heard sirens.

"He turned," said Lydia.

"He's not getting away." River flipped a U-turn and pulled his radio. "Requesting backup. This is Officer Jameson. I am in pursuit of a tan SUV close to where I live."

He didn't like that Lydia might be in danger but catching this guy might end the nightmare she'd been living in. He raced up and down side streets, catching a glimpse of the tail end of a tan vehicle. When he turned onto a new street, the car he'd been following had parked in a driveway. A mother and child got out of the car. He'd followed the wrong vehicle.

The sirens wailed through the streets. The Ridge Police Department must have sent most of their force. Maybe they would be able to track down the elusive SUV.

"You okay?"

She nodded. "Still waiting for my heart to slow down. This isn't anything you ever get used to, is it?"

"No." He let out a breath. "Let's get you to the police station. That's the safest place for you for now."

He drove slower across town. He reached over and patted her leg, hoping to calm her.

His phone, which he'd placed on the console, rang.

"It's Eva." Lydia's voice held a note of tension.

"Put her on speakerphone so we can both hear it."

Lydia pressed a button.

He leaned toward the phone. "Eva, what you got for me?"

"You're not going to believe where that phone call from Sheryl Caldwell came from."

SIXTEEN

Lydia pressed her arms against her side, laced her fingers together and bit her lower lip. What had Eva discovered?

"Go ahead," said River.

"I pinpointed the call to where that public land comes up against Gregory Larson's property."

"Are you sure? There's nothing out there. The closest structure is that clubhouse over a couple of hills. There was no indication Elsie had been there."

"It looks like the call came from between the clubhouse and the property line at the bottom of the hill," said Eva.

Lydia thought about what River had said about Elsie and her abductor appearing to have been lifted into the air. She touched River's arm. What if they hadn't gone up but *down*? The realization caused her to remember why she thought she had seen Gregory Larson in a different context other than his real estate ads.

"Eva, I think Gregory Larson might be connected to the kidnapping," she said. "Years ago, he was involved in a custody suit with his ex-wife. It was on the local news. The wife was alleging that he had extremist views because he was into survivalist thinking, stockpiling guns and stuff. What if there's a hidden bunker on his property and that's where Elsie is?"

River jerked in his seat and slowed the car down. "Lydia might be right. If the bunker is deep underground, that would explain why the dogs lost the scent."

"Give me five minutes," said Eva.

"Can you find out who on the task force is close? We need to go out and search that place again. I wonder if Gregory owns an older model tan SUV?"

"Because this is urgent, I'll drop everything and get right on this."

"Thank you, Eva." River hung up.

"That has to be it," said Lydia feeling a rising sense of hope.

"The bunker entrance must be really well concealed." His words came out in staccato rhythm, as if his thoughts were racing. "I wonder if there's a second entrance in that clubhouse."

Lydia's heart pounded. Was she finally going to hold Elsie again?

"I'll drop you off at the police station."

"That will eat up precious minutes. I'm going with you. If Elsie is hidden in those hills, I want my face to be the first one she sees."

"This could be dangerous."

"I don't care. I need to know my daughter's safe."

River shook his head. "Somehow, I don't think arguing with you is worth the energy expenditure. Hopefully, we'll have two or three more armed officers. If I say you need to hang back or stay in the car, you need to comply."

"I understand."

River took the turn that would lead them out of town. The phone rang again. Eva. Lydia pressed the connect button.

"Eli and Maren are close by. They should be able to meet you up there within a few minutes. There's no tan SUV registered to Gregory, and he's not answering his phone. I talked to his assistant in his office. She hasn't seen him in the last day, and he missed a real estate showing. She hinted that his financials are not as good as they used to be. He was heavily leveraged in a real estate venture that went belly up and his divorce cost him big-time."

"Good work," said River. "Do you think that is probable cause for us to search his property under suspicion that he's involved?"

"I'll talk to Emmett. If you had a clear link between him and either Sheryl or Norm, that might help," said Eva.

"Okay, thanks."

Lydia stared down at the phone after ending the call. "I never met Gregory before we saw him at the clubhouse. Sheryl and Norm certainly never mentioned him."

"I wonder what the connection is. Gregory had a financial need and maybe even some empathy because of his own custody battle. Did Norm like to shoot skeet?"

"I'm not sure he even owns a gun." Something clicked in her mind. "He is a member of a drone club, though. There was a guy flying a drone that day we were up there. Maybe the club utilizes Gregory's land."

"That must be it." River came to the turnoff that would lead to the dirt road and creek where the two properties connected.

As they rumbled up the dirt road, she took in a breath to try to release the tension that had invaded her muscles.

River pulled over and stopped the patrol vehicle. "Frankie and I are going to get out and have a look around while we wait for the others. You stay here in the car."

She nodded. She watched as River led his K-9 around the area while Maren and Eli pulled up and got out of their respective vehicles.

Lydia continued to sit in the car while the three officers worked the area with their K-9s. River's phone rang from where he'd left it on the console.

"Hi, Eva. It's Lydia. River's not in the car."

"Let him know that Emmett said we do have probable cause to go on the land with the cell phone call having been made from there. Where the call was made from is triangulated off of towers, so it's not exact, but I'm sending a map to his phone. It's only a short distance up the hill from the boundary between the public land and Gregory's property."

"If this bunker is deep underground, so far down that the dogs would lose the scent, wouldn't Sheryl have had to be above ground for the signal from her cell phone to work?"

"Maybe. I know mountains will often block a cell phone signal," said Eva.

Search and rescue might have called off the search by the next morning when Sheryl made the call. River had said something about the search going through the night.

Lydia grabbed the phone and pushed the door open, running over to River with the news. While the other handlers took off with their dogs, Lydia walked back and forth across a swath of land that had a lot of brush. In one spot, her footsteps sounded different. She whirled around and jumped up and down. The ground beneath her had a hollow sound.

River and Frankie walked over to her.

"I think this must be where the bunker is. Listen." She jumped up and down again.

"It could be," he said. He turned one way and then the other. "There has to have been a mechanism to open the place up for them to have disappeared so fast—"

His words were cut off by the sound of gunshots. They both dropped to the ground as did Eli and Maren. The shots were coming from downhill, where their vehicles were parked. No way could they get back to them.

More shots were fired. Lydia and River, with Frankie taking up the lead, crouched and headed for a bush that would provide a degree of cover. "We need to get out of range," said River.

The other two handlers were headed up the hill with their dogs as well. Maren and Eli moved from a cluster of trees to some brush. When Lydia glanced over her shoulder, she saw a man close to the patrol vehicles. Her breath caught. What if he disabled the vehicles? They would be on foot.

"I'm calling for police backup." River seemed to know what she was thinking.

It would take the Ridge police at least twenty minutes to get out here. Did they have that kind of time?

A shot zinged over her head. Lydia dropped to her stomach, trying to still her breathing and slow her racing heart as she lay on the hard ground. River crawled over to her.

"The others are signaling that they will hold him off if he tries to get up this mountain. He's at a disadvantage because he's downhill from us. Frankie and I need to get you to where it's safe."

They moved up the hill. The clubhouse and the skeet shooting range came into view. There were no cars parked in the dirt lot.

River stared down the hill. "I wonder..."

Behind them, more shots were fired. She prayed for the safety of the other officers. "You wonder what?"

"That fireplace in that clubhouse. It looked like it had never been used."

River and Frankie were already headed toward the clubhouse.

She ran to keep up with them.

When they got to the clubhouse, River yanked on the door. Locked. He stared at it for a long moment. "Simple lock." He pulled a credit card from his wallet and slid it between the lock and the door frame. It opened.

Their feet echoed on the wood floor in the empty space. River dropped to his knees in front of the fireplace. Out of breath from running, Lydia leaned over, resting her hands on her knees.

"Let's see what we have here," he said.

Frankie pressed close to his side as River reached into the fireplace. The back wall was not solid, just two pieces of metal that came together in the middle.

Lydia straightened. "You need something flat and strong to pry it open."

He could hear her pacing around the room and then retreating to the other rooms. She returned with a flathead screwdriver, which he pressed into the seam so he could separate the pieces of metal.

He pulled out his phone and turned on the flashlight. "Hello." He could see a concrete floor and stairs.

Lydia squeezed his shoulder. "Elsie might be down there."

"Yes, and we might be going into a firefight. Let me call Eli and let him know what we found."

He pressed Eli's number.

"Yes?" said Eli.

"We found a passageway in the fireplace of the clubhouse that might lead to a bunker. What is your situation?"

"The shooter appears to have retreated."

"Can you and Maren get up here? I'm going to check this out. Someone needs to stay with Lydia."

"Be there in five," said Eli. "I'll let Maren know."

"Sounds good."

Lydia stepped closer to him. "I'm going down there with you."

"It could be dangerous. You need to wait up here with one of the other officers."

"Elsie might be down there." Her voice held a note of urgency.

Through the window that looked out onto the range and the parking lot, River caught a flash of motion. He turned. A car he didn't recognize had pulled into the lot.

Lydia let out a breath and squeezed his arm. "What if he's been sent by Gregory Larson?"

Now Lydia might be in danger if she stayed above ground. "We'll go down the steps to hide."

River phoned Eli to let him know what was going on. After Frankie made her way down the stairs, he and Lydia followed. He slid the metal doors closed. He shone his flashlight to reveal a long concrete passageway. This had to lead to the bunker down the hill.

Lydia was already making her way along the corridor. "Hold up," he said. "We have to wait for backup."

Lydia walked briskly, as if she hadn't heard him. The compulsion to find her daughter overrode even keeping herself safe.

When he checked his cell phone, he found he had no bars meaning there was no signal once they were underground. He ran to catch up with her. They moved down the concrete hallway until they came to a set of steps off to the side.

River tilted his head. Two more metal doors, but much larger than the fireplace doors. On one side of the wall was a metal box.

Lydia opened the box. Inside was a set of buttons and switches. He pressed a green button and the doors lifted open. He hurried up the stairs and peered around. They were probably midway between the clubhouse and the boundary to Gregory's land.

"This must be where Sheryl came outside to make her phone call."

The doors had a substantial amount of dirt and grass on them, so the entrance would be concealed from anybody walking by. Through the open doors, River stood where he could get a signal and called Eli. "There's an escape hatch midway between the clubhouse and the river. We'll leave it open for you."

"Wrangler and I can get there fairly quickly. Maren and Haven are headed up to the clubhouse to question the man who just pulled up."

"We'll wait for you."

When River descended the stairs, Lydia was already making her way through the corridor, Frankie beside her.

He hurried to catch up with her. "Lydia, slow down. We don't know what we're walking into."

They came to another set of doors, this one in front of them, with another control panel. River pulled his gun. Up the hallway, he could see Eli and Wrangler approaching. The compact Malinois moved with grace.

"Stand off to the side, out of view," said River.

Lydia pressed herself close to the wall. "This could be it. My little girl could be in there."

River reached to open the control panel just as Eli caught up with them. He pulled his gun as well.

River pushed the button and the doors slid open. Inside were shelves stocked with food and water jugs, several beds and a couch. The place appeared to be empty. The two men moved inside with their dogs by their side. A narrow hallway led to a bathroom and more shelving that contained guns, ammunition and blankets.

River called to Lydia. "It's clear."

Lydia crossed the threshold. "She's not in here?"

River shook his head.

Shoulders slumped, head down, Lydia stepped into the room and gazed around. She stopped, letting out an audible breath and then rushing over to one of the beds, where she picked something up. "Elsie was here. This is her barrette."

"We were too late." River could feel the weight of failure suctioning around him all over again. If they had thought of the possibility of a bunker sooner, they might have been able to rescue Elsie right away.

Clutching the barrette in her fist, Lydia hurried over to him, patting his arm. "This is not your fault. No one could have guessed this was here."

While he appreciated her not blaming him, he could not let go of the idea that he should have figured it out about the bunker sooner.

Eli stepped up to River. "This isn't anything we've had to deal with before. All kinds of things can distort a scent for a K-9. It certainly never came up in any of our training."

Eli moved around the room. "They couldn't have made it all the way up that hill and into the clubhouse entrance without being spotted, or even to that midway spot. There must be an entrance closer to the river." He pulled back a curtain. "There's another hallway here."

Lydia crept forward. "Another room, maybe Elsie is in there."

River held her back. "Let us go first."

Both men had their guns drawn as they made their way down the short hallway to a garage-style room where the tan SUV was parked. That explained why the vehicle had simply disappeared the day they'd chased it on the dirt road. Gregory had probably bought the car from a private citizen and then never registered it so there would be no way to trace it.

River circled the vehicle and peered inside. Nothing. Fighting off his own disappointment, he looked up the hallway to where Lydia stood, a hopeful expression on her face. He shook his head, and her jaw dropped. He felt the disappointment he read on her face in the hollow of his chest.

Eli strode across the concrete floor. “There’s another control panel here.” He opened it and pressed a button.

A sort of loud yawning and creaking filled the room as metal doors weighted with dirt and grass opened wide.

River looked up in time to see Gregory Larson aiming a rifle at his chest.

SEVENTEEN

With terror coursing through her, Lydia screamed when she heard the rifle shots. More shots were fired. One dog barked and another yelped as if in pain. She couldn't see River anywhere.

Eli advanced up the hallway and grabbed her elbow. "We need to get you out of here."

She pulled away. "Where's River?"

"Come on," said Eli. Wrangler stayed close to Eli.

She still clutched Elsie's barrette as she was led up the passageway.

As they ran, she could hear the yawning sound of the huge doors closing. Where were River and Frankie?

Up ahead in the hallway, light still streamed through the midway doors where they had been left open. Eli drew his weapon and pressed his back against the concrete wall, signaling for Lydia to do the same. Lydia reached over to the control panel to shut the doors.

When she looked over her shoulder, River was moving up the hallway with Frankie. She let out the breath she'd been holding. River and Frankie were okay.

Once the doors were shut, Eli signaled for Lydia to follow.

"I'm waiting for River and Frankie," said Lydia.

"I'll go on ahead," said Eli. "Maybe we can still catch this guy."

River caught up with her.

"I heard Frankie yelp."

"I stepped on her foot in an effort to get out of the way of the gunfire when Gregory shot at me before I got the doors closed."

Frankie gave a tail wag when Lydia looked down at her. "Poor girl."

"Let's go. We need to find out where Elsie is being kept. Her grandparents might not have a close hideaway, but I bet a real estate agent with lots of empty properties might have one now that we know for sure that he's involved."

They moved along the hallway until they got to the stairs that led to the fireplace. Eli was the first to go up the stairs. He yelled back down, "I'm going to see if I can catch Gregory."

River, Lydia and Frankie made their way up the stairs.

Outside, the car that had previously pulled up was gone. Maren ran toward them. "That guy was just up here to practice fly fishing. I let him go. Ridge police are on their way."

"Elsie was kept here, but she's been moved." Lydia opened her hand to show Maren the barrette. "This was hers. This was in my little girl's hair." Her throat constricted and tears warmed her eyes.

River reached over and squeezed Lydia's arm.

"Eli's gone downhill to see if he can catch Gregory Larson." River leaned close to her as he spoke to Maren. "If we can't catch him and find out if he knows where Elsie is being kept, we need to deploy K-9s to any empty and remote properties that Gregory might be trying to sell. I'll get on the phone to Eva to see if Gregory owns a cabin or any place a child could be hidden."

Maren nodded. "If we can get back down to our vehicles, I can get on my laptop right now to see if we can narrow down the properties from his website."

"We need to wait for a word from Eli to make sure it's safe."

"Maybe I can look it up on my phone." Maren stepped a few feet away from them.

He turned in a half circle, his words coming out in a rapid-fire fashion. "I'll call Emmett to find out how many team members we can get here as quickly as possible."

River turned to Lydia. She held the barrette in her closed fist. He wrapped his arm around her. "We're going to find her before they can get her out of the country."

They were so close to ending this nightmare.

His touch warmed her and made it possible for her to take a deep breath. She gazed into his eyes. "I'm so glad you're here with me."

He pressed his hand against her cheek. "No place I'd rather be."

At the most harrowing time in her life, River had stayed with her. It spoke volumes about his character. He didn't run or hide in a bottle like Sloane had when things got hard.

River stepped away to make his phone calls.

With one hand, she stroked Frankie's head. With the other, she clutched Elsie's barrette. It was silver with fabric flowers on it. She looked at Frankie, who gazed up at her with big brown eyes. "He's all right, isn't he? That River." Frankie licked Lydia's hand. "You're pretty okay yourself."

A Ridge police cruiser pulled into the dirt parking lot.

River turned to face her. "We've narrowed it down to two properties where they might be holding Elsie. The guy has places all over the state for sale. Lizzie and Autumn are closer to the first location. Eli, Maren and I will cover the other place. It's a large log cabin on the other side of Ridge Mountain. Eli thinks that Gregory got away. The Ridge police officer will give us a ride back down to our patrol cars." He pointed toward Maren who stood with Haven.

She had never seen such a look of intensity in his eyes.

"The task force will bring her home safe." His voice held a tone of deep conviction.

She had the feeling that if it came to it, River would die in order to bring Elsie back to her.

As the three of them and the two K-9s hurried to the cruiser, Lydia's heart raced. She'd had so many disappointments since Elsie had been taken, she didn't want to get her hopes up. Still, she sensed that she was getting close to being able to hold Elsie in her arms again.

Please, Lord, I want to chase butterflies with my daughter again and receive a million more dandelion bouquets from her. Please give me that chance.

The Ridge police officer dropped Maren, Lydia and River off at their vehicles. Eli must have already left by the time they got there. Maren loaded up Haven and sped away. The Ridge patrol officer lingered while River let Frankie do her business. The police officer pulled away as River moved to load Frankie. He had just settled Frankie into her kennel when a strange buzzing sound reached his ears.

Lydia's hand was on the door handle. "What is that noise?"

The Ridge police officer had gone out of sight around a curve.

Gunshots from the air peppered the earth around them. River caught a glimpse of the drone above them right before he hit the ground. He rolled underneath his patrol car as more shots surrounded him. Lydia pressed in beside him.

With his heart pounding, he moved to the edge of the car and peered up. The drone was just making a turn to come back and fire at them again. "Get in the car!"

Lydia responded immediately. River rolled his body across the dirt. He had a momentary view of the sky before he flipped over on his stomach. The drone was getting closer. He reached for the door handle and flung it open. Bullets hit the top of the car.

As he turned the key in the ignition, he saw that the drone had dropped down so it could shoot through the windows of the patrol car. Lydia slumped down in her seat. He floored the accelerator, kicking up dirt as he headed toward the mountain road.

He heard the ping of a bullet hitting metal.

"He's there. I saw him in the trees." Either Gregory had run out of bullets for his rifle or the drone was a better way to guarantee a more accurate shot. Norm must have taught him about the drones, just like Gregory had probably loaned Norm a gun when they had been shot at from the front and back of his house.

He stopped the car but left it idling. River's gaze jerked around, taking in segments of the evergreens on Lydia's side of the road. He didn't see anything. No sign of movement or color that didn't blend into the trees. "You sure?"

"A face. I saw a face." She pointed at an evergreen that looked like it had been split by lightning. "By that tree."

The drone operator would have had to be close enough to operate with a view on its target, unless the drone had some sort of camera on it. He radioed the Ridge police officer, who would still be close, for backup.

River pressed the button that automatically opened Frankie's kennel at the same time he pushed open the door. He didn't need to tell Lydia to stay in the patrol car.

Frankie jumped down from the car and caught up with River, who had already drawn his gun and was running toward the trees. He couldn't see or hear the drone anymore.

Fully aware that the man had a rifle, he sought shelter behind some brush. When no shots were fired, he sprinted forward to the next place that would provide cover. Maybe Gregory was out of bullets. Frankie pressed in close to his side. He studied the area by the split tree.

River stepped out into the open. Still no shots or sign of anyone lurking in the trees. Sunlight caught a glint of metal. The drone lying on the ground.

His heart squeezed tight. He raised his gun and moved in. Frankie turned slightly and let out a warning bark.

Off to the side, River heard a rustling noise. He'd only made a half turn when a rifle butt collided with his head. His knees buckled and he collapsed to the ground. The sound of Frankie's frantic barking and someone's retreating footsteps pummeled his ears.

Gregory was headed toward where Lydia sat in the car. It had been his intention all along to get at her.

As he fought not to pass out and get to his feet, River prayed that Gregory would not succeed in his mission.

EIGHTEEN

Lydia watched in horror as Gregory ran toward the patrol car. He held a rifle. She hadn't yet buckled herself in. She fell on her stomach, out of view, bracing for the sonic boom that would shatter the windshield.

A tense silence coiled around her, but no shot was fired. She took in several ragged breaths before lifting her head above the dashboard. Frankie was running circles around Gregory, diving in and nipping at him while he tried to hit her with the rifle. River moved in with his gun drawn. She gasped when Gregory lifted the rifle to hit River. Frankie dove for Gregory's pant leg and shook it so vigorously that it threw him off balance. He dropped the rifle and fell on his behind. Frankie moved in close to the fallen man and continued to bark.

River drew out his handcuffs and secured Gregory lifting him to his feet.

Once she was sure she wasn't in danger, Lydia pushed open the door and ran to Gregory, grabbing his collar. "Where is Elsie? What have you done with her? Where is my daughter?"

With his hands cuffed behind his back, the man could only angle away from her.

"Lydia." River wrapped his arm around her waist, lifted her up and pulled her back. "I'll question him."

Lydia gasped for air. River kept hold of her until her body relaxed.

"Sorry." Her voice grew soft as she narrowed her eyes at Gregory. "What have you done with my little girl?"

The man jutted his chin. "They told me what an unfit mother you were. Kid deserves better, just like my kid did."

"It's not true." Tears streamed down Lydia's face. "They lied."

"I'm sure there was a big payday for you, too," said River.

"So what if there was?" said Gregory.

River's phone rang. Frankie sat at attention. Her butt lifted off the ground every time the suspect twitched. Fear came into Gregory's eyes when he watched the dog. He wasn't going anywhere with the yellow Lab standing guard.

With his eyes still on the suspect, River answered his phone, speaking in low tones.

Lydia's hands balled into fists as she looked at the man who had tried to kill her more than once. "Where's my daughter?"

Gregory turned his head and looked off to the side, his jaw taut.

As she stared at him, she prayed for self-control.

River addressed his comment to Lydia. "That was Lizzie. There was nothing at the property she and Autumn went to." He stepped up to Gregory. "Is Elsie being kept at the cabin you're selling on the other side of Ridge Mountain?" Maren and Eli must be partway there by now.

Gregory pressed his tongue to the inside of his cheek and raised his eyebrows in defiance.

Maternal anger coursed through Lydia.

"Have they already left the country?" Lydia could barely get the words out.

River stepped even closer to the suspect. "Look, I contacted a Ridge police officer who's close. He's going to come and take you into the police station, where we can question you all day and night."

Tension knotted at the back of Lydia's neck. They didn't have that kind of time.

"Just tell us," said Lydia.

River held up his hand, indicating she needed to stop, then he looked at Gregory. "You're looking at several attempted murder charges. If you cooperate now, I'm sure the judge will keep that in mind when it comes to sentencing."

Gregory pressed his lips together.

Lydia had to take a step back and turn away. She didn't trust herself enough not to charge at him again. Her whole body was shaking.

"Probably going to be some kidnapping charges, too."

"I had nothing to do with that. The old lady stayed with the kid while Norm drove the car away to make it look like they'd left the area."

"You provided Sheryl and Elsie a place to hide. That makes you complicit."

Gregory's gaze darted around, as if he was considering what River had said.

Lydia gritted her teeth and closed her eyes. The man was going to jail no matter what. Why was he being so stubborn?

Up the road, the Ridge patrol vehicle came into sight.

River's phone rang again. "Eli, what did you find?"

She watched as River listened to the response. His body language told her everything she needed to know. Elsie wasn't at the cabin on Ridge Mountain.

Lydia prayed for peace that was beyond the strong emotions raging through her.

River ended the call.

A calm washed over Lydia as she stepped toward the man who knew where her daughter was. "Please." Tears streamed down her face. "Please," she whispered.

The Ridge police officer came to a stop.

Lydia persisted. "What if this was your child? You can imagine what I've been going through."

Gregory's expression softened as he stared at Lydia for a long moment before speaking. "They're at the defunct outlet mall on the old highway outside of Ridge."

"That property wasn't on your website." River shifted his weight.

"I haven't officially gotten the contract to list it. I just knew it was vacant. I didn't want this to be traced back to me. I'm in debt up to my ears. Once I did my part, I was supposed to get a big paycheck."

Lydia shuddered, knowing that Gregory's "part" was to kill her.

"You better hurry. They're planning on driving out of state tonight to an airport. They knew you'd be watching the Colorado airports."

"What airport?"

"I don't know."

The police officer approached them.

As he was led away, Gregory angled around, shouting back at River, "You'll let the DA know I cooperated?"

River waved his hand and nodded in response. He turned toward Lydia. "Let's get out there. You can call the other members of the task force on the way."

The sky had already turned gray. They didn't have much time before Sheryl and Norm left with Elsie under the cover of night.

* * *

As they drove toward the outlet mall, River knew that his colleagues were not far behind him. The mall had been built in anticipation of a bigger highway going through this part of Colorado. Growth had turned in a different direction and the mall had gone bankrupt.

By the time he took the turn that would lead to the building, the sky had grown dark. They passed several warehouses and then drove past open fields.

"I remember that mall being quite large. How are we ever going to find her?"

"I still have Elsie's coat in my car. The dogs will get a scent off that easy. We'll find her."

"Do you remember at your house? There were two people shooting at us. Norm must have gotten a gun from Gregory."

He had thought of that, too. "Yeah, Gregory must have given him some lessons."

The mall came into view, just a dark silhouette of a long, narrow building. When he peered in his rearview mirror, he saw headlights behind him. He would not be going into this alone. He glanced over at Lydia, whose jaw was set. She'd laced her fingers together. When she looked at him, he saw total trust in her eyes.

He hoped that trust was not misplaced just like it had been with Noah's mom.

As he drew closer to the parking lot, he slowed and turned off his headlights. Norm or Sheryl might be watching. There were no cars in the parking lot and the building was dark. The two cars behind him had turned off their headlights as well and had rolled into the far corner of the lot where he'd parked.

Tension suctioned his chest. The deep breath he took to relax seemed to get stuck in his lungs.

He reached over and put his hand on hers. She turned slightly and leaned toward him, resting her hand on his cheek. His lips pressed against hers then he rested his forehead against hers.

"Stay safe," she whispered.

He could smell her floral perfume as the warmth of her hand permeated his skin. Her touch and her closeness gave him courage.

He straightened and stared through the windshield. The total darkness of the facility and the fact that he didn't see a car anywhere was concerning. He hoped they weren't too late. Not a thought he would vocalize to Lydia.

He squeezed her shoulder before opening his door and then deploying Frankie and grabbing Elsie's coat. The other handlers were already waiting in the parking lot. With Frankie heeling by his side, he ran over to them.

"Two to the inside, moving in opposite directions, and one on the perimeter," said River.

"Haven and I will take the outside," said Maren.

After allowing the K-9s to get the scent off the coat, they moved toward what had been the main entrance of the mall at the center of the building. Evidence of vandalism was everywhere, broken windows, trash and graffiti. Eli and River entered the building and split off. To prevent detection, they'd be searching in the darkness relying on the dogs' noses.

No surprise that Frankie picked up on Elsie's scent right away. The child may have been all through the facility, which meant they might be running in circles for a while. A noise in one of the smaller stores caused them to turn down a side corridor. Once at the threshold, River pressed against a wall and listened. More noise, a sort of rushing sound. He heard one object colliding with another. He angled his body so he could peer in with one eye. A light breeze from a broken window ruffled some papers on a broken shelf. Frankie growled and lurched.

"Stay."

A moving shadow on a high shelf indicated the source of Frankie's ire. A raccoon scrambled down and disappeared through the broken window.

River let out the breath he'd been holding before heading back to the main corridor. They moved past a chair with no cushion laying on its side and more garbage and debris.

Frankie pulled hard when they came to a large store filled with broken display cases and empty clothing racks. Hangers and trash cluttered the floor. River stepped on broken glass, which made a crunching noise. He stopped and listened.

Frankie moved forward, padding silently. She alerted at the closed door of what must have been used for storage or a break room. He pulled a treat from his pocket as a reward for her.

River stared at the closed door. He didn't hear any sound inside.

Though all the task force members had grabbed their shoulder radios, he dare not use it for fear of giving himself away. If someone was inside, he assumed there was no other exit.

Taking in a deep breath, River pulled his weapon and reached for the doorknob. Frankie wiggled her butt with a laser focus on River as she waited for a command.

He twisted the nob and pushed the door open with his gun raised. "Police."

No rustling sound or voices reached his ears. No one was in the room. As his eyes adjusted to the dark, he saw why Frankie had alerted so strongly. There were two cots and sleeping bags, children's toys and books, as well as some boxes of ready-to-eat food. This must be where they'd kept Elsie. She would have trusted her grandparents and maybe they had found a way to make a game out of why they were in such a place.

Still, he wondered if Elsie had asked about her mother, maybe even cried over her not being with her. The notion was like a stab to his heart.

He moved back out into the wide corridor that led to the display floor of the store. A shuffling noise and then moving shadows caused him to lift his head and stare into the darkness. Frankie emitted a low growl.

Nanoseconds before the first shot was fired at him, River pressed against the wall. Frankie sounding the alarm had saved his life. The dog slipped in close to him. Two more shots were fired in his direction.

Still staying close to the wall, River raised his gun and moved toward where the shots had come from. The sound of his own breathing augmented the silence as he listened for any noise that might indicate the shooter's location. Eli would hear the shots and come running with Wrangler. They'd be able to trap Norm.

River scanned the darkness for any sign of Norm. It had to be him who had the gun. That meant Sheryl was probably with Elsie.

His phone vibrated loudly in his pocket. Probably Lydia wanting an update.

Even though the phone was on vibrate, he heard retreating footsteps. The noise had been enough to alarm Norm. No time to answer it. He and Frankie raced through the store toward the corridor that connected to all the empty stores, moving in the direction he'd heard the footsteps.

On high alert, he stayed close to the wall, watching and

listening as he scanned the entire area. There were a hundred nooks and storefronts Norm could have slipped into.

At the other end of the corridor, he spotted Eli and Wrangler making their way up toward him.

He saw the muzzle flash right before he heard the bullet leave the chamber.

Shots resounded, breaking the glass storefront behind him and raining glass down upon him. He put his arms up to protect himself. Another shot caused him to grip his arm where he felt a radiating and intense sting. He'd been grazed.

He dropped to the floor just as another shot whizzed toward him. Gripping his arm, he sought the cover of an overturned chair before lifting his gun to fire back, praying that the bullet found its target.

NINETEEN

Lydia's heart pounded erratically as she stared at the phone. River had not answered her call. She'd seen two people come out of the mall and move toward the trees. There had been enough moonlight to discern that one shadowy figure was smaller and shorter than the other.

She didn't have the phone numbers of the other officers. There was no time. Sheryl was probably escaping with Elsie. She pushed open the door and ran to where the two people had disappeared into the trees.

The parking lot was filled with cracks and bumps as her feet pounded on the concrete, and she leaped around garbage, twisted metal and a mattress. The canopy of the trees made the night even darker. Sheryl had not been carrying a flashlight. She would have to move slowly with Elsie.

Her heartbeat drummed in her ears as she treaded the undergrowth of the forest. She stepped where there seemed to be a sort of path.

She heard a scream. Elsie's scream.

Lydia shot through the forest toward the sound of her daughter in distress. The trees thinned. She saw a car in the distance, parked in an open area but concealed from the road by brush.

Though she could not see her, the sound of Elsie's crying

compelled Lydia forward. She pushed through the trees and brush. Then she saw it. Elsie lying on the ground caught in a tangle of undergrowth. Sheryl was bent over her.

Sheryl's head shot up. Lydia had been spotted. Sheryl could run and get away in the car if she left Elsie behind. Instead, she reached for her granddaughter, making soothing sounds as she sought to free the child's legs from the roots and branches she'd gotten tangled in.

Lydia ran to her daughter. "Elsie. Elsie."

"Mommy."

The girl fell into Lydia's arms. She held her close as tears flowed.

"She's my son's daughter," Sheryl hissed, stretching to take Elsie.

"Sheryl Caldwell, get away from the child and put your hands in the air."

Lydia glanced off to the side, where Maren stood with Haven, her gun drawn.

Sheryl turned to run toward the car. Maren shouted a command at Haven, who caught up with Sheryl and leaped at her while barking.

Sheryl put her arms in the air. "I'll stop. Just call your dog off."

Lydia looked up at the older woman and held the crying Elsie even tighter. "She's *my* daughter."

"Norm says Sloane will be a good father once he stops drinking. He can quit more easily if you're not around."

Sheryl's thinking was twisted. She'd believe anything to see their son as not at fault. Or that the pressure Norm put on his son to succeed contributed to his drinking.

Maren moved in to handcuff Sheryl. "I'm going to put her in my patrol car."

"Sure. Give me a minute with Elsie," said Lydia.

Maren led Sheryl away through the trees, her dog keeping an intent eye on the suspect.

Lydia rose to her feet, still holding Elsie close. "My precious, precious girl." She brushed her hand over Elsie's soft curls. "Mommy's treasure." She touched Elsie's cheek. "Are you hurt? Did Grandma give you enough to eat?"

"Yes, Grandma gave me lots of treats and toys, but Mommy, they wouldn't let me see you. They said you were bad and that they had to take me away." She wrapped her arms around her mom's neck. "I knew it wasn't true."

"No, sweetheart. Grandma and Grandpa…they were just…misguided."

"That's a big word." Elsie twirled a strand of her mother's auburn hair. Her face was close enough to Lydia's that she could feel the child's soft breath on her skin.

"I hope you weren't scared."

Elsie shook her head then patted her mom's cheek. "I missed you."

"Oh, baby girl, you have no idea how much I missed you." She put Elsie on the ground and then took her hand. "Come on, we're going to go sit in a policeman's car."

"Is he a nice policeman?"

"Yes, he's very nice indeed and he has a really sweet dog."

"A dog." Elsie squealed with delight. "Can I pet the dog and give her hugs?"

Lydia thought her heart would burst at the sound of her daughter's voice. Her daughter was safe. Her excitement about the dog indicated that maybe she had not been overly traumatized. Lydia knew though that there would still be much to process. The important thing right now was that Elsie was back in her arms.

As they came to the edge of the forest, she could see Maren putting Sheryl in her patrol car.

Gunfire, at least five shots, came from within the mall. One of the windows lit up from the volley.

Lydia grabbed Elsie and pulled her close praying that River and Eli were okay. A second later, Norm emerged from the building. Her heart pounded as she picked up Elsie. She needed to get to the patrol car before Norm could get to her.

With Frankie running ahead, River chased after Norm as he exited the building and ran for the trees. When shots had been fired in his direction, Eli had retreated, but River knew he would take up the pursuit.

Off to the side, he caught a glimpse of Lydia holding a child, running toward the patrol car to get away from where Norm had gone. Even as he focused on taking down Norm, his heart burst with joy to know that Elsie was with her mother.

He could hear Norm as he crashed through the forest then disappeared from view. The pain radiating through River's injured arm slowed him down. He kept running, brushing branches out of his way with his good arm while he held the gun with his injured arm. He and Frankie burst through the trees to an open area. Norm was behind the wheel of a car. River leveled his gun to fire off a shot before the car was out of range and had reached a road.

River pressed the talk button on his shoulder radio. "He's getting away through the trees." He could see the red glow of the taillights. "To the east, not the road we came in on."

"I'm at my patrol vehicle now," said Maren. "Sheryl is in custody. I can chase him."

The radio disconnected and then he heard the sound of

a car peeling out. Feeling the strength draining from him, he stumbled back through the trees. He was bent over and gripping his arm by the time he stepped onto the parking lot.

Lydia came toward him. "You're hurt."

He heard a small voice that was music to his ears. "Mommy, is this the nice policeman?"

"Yes, this is River and his dog Frankie."

Even though his injury caused great pain, River reached a hand out toward Elsie. "It's nice to meet you, Elsie. I'm River." The child had the same sweet smile as her mother. He'd like to see more of those smiles.

Elsie did a little curtsey. "Nice to meet you." The girl drew her attention to the yellow Lab wagging her tail.

"This is Frankie?" Seeing delight in the child's eyes as she moved to pet the dog eased some of River's pain.

Lydia wrapped her arm around River's back, gripping his good shoulder. "You need to go to a hospital."

He nodded through gritted teeth. "Can't argue with you there."

She helped him to the passenger side of the patrol car. Eli was already pulling out, maybe to help Maren with the pursuit.

Lydia drove River to the ER to be taken care of while she had Elsie checked out as well. Once his wound had been cleaned and bandaged and the doctor had prescribed painkillers, he made his way down the hall to the waiting room where Lydia and Elsie sat. Taking on the role of protector, Frankie rested at Elsie's feet.

Maren entered the ER waiting room, looked around and moved toward River.

"We weren't able to catch Norm. We've got a BOLO out for him," said Maren.

River's gut clenched. Norm was still out there.

He patted his colleague's arm. "I know you did your best. Has anyone questioned Sheryl to find out where he might be?"

"I did when we took her into the Ridge police station. She didn't know where he would go, but it's clear he was the mastermind behind this whole thing. In the course of the interview, my impression was that Sheryl was a bit of shrinking violet who went along with whatever her husband said."

"That sounds about right," said Lydia.

River had one eye on Elsie as she grabbed a book from a table and lay down beside Frankie, using the dog's stomach as a pillow. The scene warmed his heart.

"In any case," said Maren, "we need to keep Lydia and Elsie safe."

"My house might be one of the first places they'll look and my windows still aren't fixed anyway."

"I'll talk to Emmett and see if he can arrange a safe house."

"In the meantime, maybe it would be best if I took them to a hotel and kept watch. I'll see if the Ridge PD can provide additional protection."

"That sounds good. I'm sure you'll want some time for that arm to recover."

"Keep me in the loop about Mia's case," said River.

"For sure. I'll follow you to the hotel."

River went to Lydia to explain the situation. Norm was still out there and seemed bent on taking Elsie and ending Lydia's life.

TWENTY

Lydia stared around at the cabin where she and Elsie had stayed with River and Frankie for two days. The cabin consisted of two bedrooms and a large room that served as a living room and kitchen. From the bedroom where she and Elsie slept, she could hear River playing with Elsie and Frankie in the living room. She smoothed the blankets over the bed. They'd only had time to grab a few things for Elsie from Lydia's house on the way to the cabin, but River had been coming up with games for Elsie to play ever since they'd come here. Keeping a three-year-old child inside and out of sight was proving to be a challenge, but River seemed to be up to it. Unfortunately, Elsie seemed to have grown used to confinement. Frankie let out a happy-sounding yip.

Lydia entered the living room and kitchen area where River had twisted together what looked like a makeshift tug toy for Frankie. She stared down at one of the long-sleeved shirts River had brought with him, which no longer had any sleeves. He must have braided the sleeves together to make the toy.

"Wasn't that one of the new shirts we got at the store before we came out here?"

"I can still wear it." He turned his attention back to Frankie. "I think we needed this more. Dog and child were getting restless."

Elsie squealed with delight as Frankie tugged and growled. She clapped her hands. "Let me do it."

River handed Elsie the tug toy, cupping her hand and placing it in her palm. Elsie waved the toy up and down until Frankie took it. The dog seemed to adjust to Elsie having less strength than River, tugging lightly.

The picture of the three of them together warmed Lydia's heart. River seemed to have a natural ability to connect with children. Or maybe it was just that he connected with Elsie.

Lydia hurried over to the kitchen. "Elsie, are you getting hungry? I'll make us a snack."

"Sure, Mama."

"I need to take Frankie out for her potty break anyway."

River headed outside with Frankie. From the kitchen window, she watched River head down a trail. This cabin was one of three that looked out on a lake and was used by the police to keep witnesses safe. The other two cabins were not occupied. At night, a Ridge police officer was parked outside.

Lydia was beginning to wonder if Norm had just decided to save himself and leave the country. She longed for her and Elsie to get back to their home and normal life. She opened a package of crackers.

Elsie moved toward the table. "I think Mr. Binkins would like a snack, too."

Lydia set the crackers on the table along with a box juice. "I'll go get him. You get started on your snack."

Mr. Binkins had always been a source of comfort to Elsie and she was glad she'd thought to grab the teddy bear.

She picked the bear up off the bed and returned to the kitchen. She stuttered in her step as shock spread through her. The door was open, and Elsie was gone. Heart pounding, Lydia ran outside in time to see Norm feet away from a car that was partially hidden by another cabin.

She ran toward her daughter.

Norm turned around and fired a gun in her direction.

From the lake where he'd been letting Frankie get some exercise, a child's faint scream reached River's ears. Had he even heard right? He scrambled up the trail. The sound of a gunshot made his stomach lurch. He couldn't believe that Norm had found them. After so many days, he'd begun to think Norm had fled to save himself. In response to the gunfire, he pulled out his own weapon. With Frankie by his side, he burst through the trees in time to see Lydia lying on the ground.

She lifted her head and pointed. He heard the sound of a car starting up but didn't see it until it pulled out from behind one of the other cabins.

Adrenaline surged. He could see Elsie through the window on the passenger side. Her hands pressed against the glass. Fear etched in her features. He couldn't risk hitting her to take out Norm.

He aimed for the tires, shooting twice.

Norm did a sudden turn, zooming toward him. He heard Lydia scream as he jumped out of the way.

He sprinted toward Norm's car as it reached the edge of the parking area, firing off three more shots. The car pulled out onto the dirt road. Frankie kept pace with him as he ran through a field to try to cut the car off.

He fired more shots, two at the engine and two more at the tires. He had to stop Norm. The car disappeared around a corner. He kept running. When he got around the curve, River didn't see the car. He wasn't about to give up. His bullets must have disabled the vehicle in some way.

He heard a car behind him. Lydia in the patrol car. He swung open the passenger's-side door, commanding Frankie to jump in. Lydia pressed the gas before he'd even closed the door, a look of hard-rock determination on her face.

She floored it, causing the back end to fishtail. She rounded another curve. Up ahead, Norm's car was on the side of the road. Steam rolled out of the engine. They got to the car and jumped out. River held his gun. "Stay back. Let me check it out."

The car was empty, and the passenger's door had been left open. When he glanced across the narrow field by the road, he saw Norm, carrying Elsie, stepping into the trees. Frankie had already taken off across the field. He followed with Lydia close behind him.

When River entered the trees, Frankie had disappeared. Erratic and intense barking reached his ears. With his gun still drawn, he rushed toward the sound.

Frankie circled Norm, who had set a frightened Elsie down. The dog growled and leapt at Norm as he raised his gun to shoot.

"Don't you dare." River had Norm in his sight. "Drop the gun."

Frankie was still circling and lunging toward Norm.

"Get your dog to back off."

"Drop the gun and I will."

Norm complied, lifting his hands in the air. River commanded Frankie to stop. The dog sat back on her haunches, but her behind was not on the ground, as if she was ready to spring at any moment.

Norm looked sideways at the dog, clearly fazed by the near attack.

Lydia came through the trees and ran to her daughter, scooping her up and holding her close as she glared at Norm. "This is not how a grandfather acts."

"You should've been a better wife. You drove him to

drink." Norm's voice faltered. "Sloane was devastated when you got sole custody. We just thought if he could have his child back…maybe he'd get his life back on track."

River saw in that moment how distorted Norm's thinking was and how a parent's love could become so twisted.

Crying, Elsie snuggled close to her mother's neck as Lydia walked back toward River, who moved in to handcuff Norm.

After River called for another patrol car, he marched Norm through the trees and secured him in his car.

River, Frankie, Elsie and Lydia waited on the side of the road.

Lydia's hand slipped into his. "It's over. Thanks to you and Frankie."

Elsie had come around to his other side. Her little hand slipped into his. She tilted her head up toward him. "Thank you, River. Grandpa was bad."

He stared down into trusting green eyes, just like her mother's. "He won't ever scare you again."

"Promise," said Elsie.

"I promise." As he stood with both his hands being held, he thought that this was the most loved he'd ever felt.

Love? Was that what he was feeling?

Once the other patrol car came to get Norm, River drove to the cabin to get the few things they had there and then headed for Ridge. He'd texted Emmett that Norm was in custody. Emmett texted back right away, congratulating him and asking him if he could be at the Denver FBI office within the hour. Now he'd be able to put his full attention on Mia's case and finding the culprits who were killing young women.

He stopped in front of Lydia's house. Elsie was in the back seat with Frankie.

Lydia stared at her house. "I can't believe we get to go back to our home, Elsie girl."

"Thanks to the nice policeman." From her car seat where she sat in the backseat of the car, Elsie raised her arms in the air.

Lydia locked River in her gaze. "Yes, thanks to the nice policeman."

The intensity of the affection he saw in her eyes made his heart flutter at the same time fear entered his awareness. "I'll walk you two to your door."

Lydia unlocked the door. The kitchen still showed damage from the blast that had probably been Norm's doing. The rest of the interior was undamaged except for a burnt smell that hung in the air.

Elsie ran inside screaming, "Hello, beautiful house." Her gaze rested momentarily on the damaged kitchen.

Lydia laid her hand on Elsie's shoulder. "We have a little bit of fixing up to do."

Seeming to shake off her confusion about the kitchen, Elsie came back to the open door, pressing her foot against her calf and tilting her head. "Can Frankie come in and see my room?"

Lydia glanced nervously at River. "I think that she and River have to get back to work, right?"

River studied her for a long moment, memorizing every freckle on her face and the way the light danced in her eyes. "Right."

It would be good to feel like he was fully contributing to the task force mission, but he found himself not wanting to leave Lydia and Elsie. Seeing Frankie interact with the little girl who had such an affinity with animals made the burdens he bore seem lighter.

Elsie disappeared inside the house.

Lydia reached out and touched his arm. "Well, I better go."

He nodded. She fell into his arms, wrapping her arms around his neck. "Thank you for everything." Having her so close warmed him to his marrow.

A tiny arm wrapped around his leg and Elsie stared up at him.

Lydia pulled free of the hug and picked Elsie up. "Come on, Pumpkin, we got to let River and Frankie get back to work."

River made his way down the walkway to his car. When he looked through the window as he pulled away, Lydia and Elsie were still standing on the porch, waving.

Frankie whimpered from her kennel.

"I agree, girl, those are two of the most loving people I've ever known."

As he drove to the edge of Ridge and took the exit that would lead him to Denver, thirty minutes away, a hollow feeling settled into his bones. Maybe it was just because the case was over. There was always a sense of floundering once an investigation wrapped up. Though he was overjoyed that Elsie was safe and home the feeling was bittersweet knowing that Noah would never be returned to his mom. He had come to realize that the nature of police work could be both heartbreaking and victorious. All of it was in God's hands.

His car clipped past the sign that said Denver was getting closer.

This feeling was different somehow than just seeing a case to a close. Even as he parked by the FBI facility where Emmett worked and where there was a training center for the K-9s, he couldn't shake the emptiness he'd felt since he'd pulled away from Lydia house.

TWENTY-ONE

River, Eli and Maren sat at the conference table with Emmett at the head of it. The dogs had been left in kennels at the training center.

"I think everyone who can be here is." Emmett glanced over at the screen where Lizzie's and Autumn's heads were visible along with Trevor Slate, a tall, dark-eyed officer who lived near Colorado Springs.

Emmett spoke up. "We're glad to have River fully onboard now that Elsie has been returned safe and sound to her mother."

Several of the officers whispered congratulations.

"I couldn't have done it without everyone's help," said River.

Emmett cleared his throat. "It's always good when a child is found safe. That having been said, I need to give everyone an update on where we are with the baby trafficking case. New information has come in that will determine the direction of our investigation. The clock is ticking for finding Mia, so we need to move on this."

"I'm glad to be back and able to give a hundred percent," said River. Maybe if he focused on this investigation, he could shake the intense sense of loss that he felt.

"Glad to have you on board," said Trevor from the screen.

Emmett shuffled the papers in front of him. "As you

all know, we've been homing in on the free clinics here in Denver because we know that Gayle Gorman visited one."

From the screen, Lizzie spoke up. "We questioned the staff at each of the clinics to see if they recognized Gayle or the other two victims."

Autumn spoke from the screen as well. "We also wanted to know if staff remembered anyone approaching any of the young women who frequented the clinic, offering to help them."

"Did you pinpoint the clinic where Gayle went?" River shifted his weight in his chair as the memory of Lydia and Elsie hugging him floated through his brain.

"Yes," said Emmett.

"But she only went there once," added Lizzie.

"One of the leads that I need to advise you all of is that, in the course of questioning staff at that same clinic, a receptionist remembered a high-end silver SUV with a man and a woman sitting inside. It struck her as odd because the two of them never got out of the vehicle. They sat there for quite a while. She's pretty sure no one came to the SUV, either."

River tried to focus on what Emmett was saying, but the memory of Lydia and Elsie holding his hands flashed through his mind. "So, like they were watching the parking lot and who was coming and going from the clinic?"

"Exactly," said Emmett. "The receptionist didn't have a clear view of the two of them and could only say that the man had light blond hair."

"That's not much to go on," said River. "No license plate or anything?"

"I did that interview," said Lizzie. "The receptionist only brought up the SUV when pressed about unusual things happening in the last few months. What struck her as off was the amount of time they were in the parking lot. The only thing she was sure about where the SUV was concerned was the color."

Trevor ran his fingers through his tousled brown hair. "So, no one at any of the local clinics where the respective victims lived recognized Gayle or Jenny or Nina? Only this one free clinic here in Denver?"

Emmett shook his head. "These girls may not have been seeking medical attention because of the shame they felt or the expense. They may have been snatched off the street just like Mia was."

"Jordan said that his sister Jenny never said if she was getting medical help, though he encouraged her to do so," said Autumn. Because of her engagement to the first victim's half brother, this case was deeply personal to the blond K-9 officer.

"Dodger told us that his wife took Mia to her OB/GYN appointments, but it wasn't at a free clinic." Emmett shook his head. "I can't emphasize enough how much this is tearing Dodger and Clara up. The one blessing is that he shared with me that Mia had started attending church with them and was really leaning hard on her newfound faith."

"At least that's something," said River. "So where is our focus going to be? Finding the SUV with so little to go on or the people inside feels like a rabbit trail."

"It's just something to keep in mind," said Emmett. "It could mean nothing, and it could be the key to this case. We're still dealing with a lot of puzzle pieces."

River wondered about the two people in the SUV. Could they be the nurse and doctor who performed the deliveries or was someone else involved who watched clinics for vulnerable pregnant women?

Emmett spoke up. "Just as a reminder, Eva is combing databases right now to give the task force some leads on medical personnel who may have lost their license or otherwise have a reason to engage in illegal activity. Once we pull up some possibilities, I'll send a couple of officers out to question known associates and colleagues at the medical facilities where they worked."

"And what about Erin and Edward McGrath, that couple that adopted a baby and then left the country without explanation? We still need to find the three babies who were already born," said Maren. "Any news on them?"

River's jaw clenched. Maren's question reminded him that vulnerable infants still needed to be found.

"We're still trying to find them for questioning." After Emmett spoke, he wrapped up the meeting.

On her way out the door, Maren put her hand on River's shoulder. "Eli and I are headed down to get our partners and check out the new K-9 trainees, why don't you come with us?"

River rose from his chair.

As they made their way down the hallway to the stairwell, Maren commented, "You seemed a little distracted in there."

"Did I?" He opened the door so Maren could go ahead of him down the stairs. Was it that obvious that he couldn't get Elsie and Lydia out of his head?

Eli was behind them on the stairs. "I noticed that, too. You asked good questions, but you kept staring out the window, like something was on your mind."

River didn't know if it was a good thing or bad thing that the other task force members were tuned in to what was going on with him.

Once inside the facility, they found the lead trainer, Dev Singh, working two German shepherd puppies through an agility course. Dev was a tall, fit man with salt-and-pepper hair and a beard. Already a grandfather, he was set to retire soon, and the facility was looking at three candidates to replace him, all of whom had excellent qualifications.

Each candidate had someone connected to the task force rooting for them. Christian Dane was Emmett's cousin. Though their relationship had been strained, Emmett was trying to remedy that. Emmett didn't have much family since his mother had been found, strangled, in a river when he was only eighteen. His mother's drowning was the reason Emmett had chosen water rescue with his Newfoundland, Gemma, as his K-9 specialty. The other two candidates were Tanya Fielding, who worked at the facility and was Dev's protégé, and Jacob Wexley, who was a friend of Dodger's.

One of the German shepherd puppies made his way over a hurdle and up a ramp. The pup focused on Dev when he gave a hand command. That must be Chance, the dog who had been doing well in the program. The other puppy barked at some unseen foe and then lay down inside a tunnel.

Maren reached in the tunnel and lifted the dog out. "You must be Trooper. I heard you had focusing issues." The pup offered her doggy kisses as his little body wiggled.

"I don't know about that guy," said Dev. "Great personality but totally doesn't have the drive we like to see in K-9s."

Chance finished the course and sat looking up at Dev, who tossed him a snack. "I'm thinking this guy might be good at suspect apprehension."

"It's still early in training." River stepped over to where Maren still held Trooper as he snuggled against her neck. "This guy still might turn things around."

"Sure," said Eli. "Dogs can change patterns of behavior just like people can."

Eli's words sank in. Ever since Noah's death, River had seen himself as unworthy of keeping a child safe. With that fear driving his actions, he'd put up a barrier to ever thinking he could have a child of his own. Maybe his pattern of thinking needed to change.

Dev excused himself, calling after the puppies to follow. Even though Maren put Trooper down, he had to be called three times before he lined up behind his brother. The pups were still too small for their big paws and floppy ears. Trooper had one ear that was still crooked.

"Dog's grow and change, don't they?" River's voice drifted off as he thought again about why Lydia and Elsie were foremost in his mind. "They can learn and grow and so can people." Lost in thought, River's voice drifted off. Could he change the way he viewed himself?

Maren stood on the other side of him. "You gonna tell us what's on your mind?"

River's cheeks heated. "It's Lydia and Elsie. The case is over, but I can't seem to get them out of my head."

"You care about them?"

Maybe more, thought River. *Maybe I love them.* "I spent so much time with Lydia under such trying circumstances. She's an incredible lady."

Maren leaned in and tapped her elbow against his arm. "So maybe there is something worth exploring between you two."

"It seems to me that if you feel something for her, you shouldn't just walk away." His voice swelled with emotion as he stepped closer to River. "When you find true love, you need to hold on tight to it."

Eli, of all people, understood immense loss.

"Yeah, maybe you're right." The three of them walked over to the kennels to get their respective dogs. Being with Lydia meant loving Elsie, too, and protecting them both from whatever life threw their way. He had a lot to think about.

* * *

"Elsie, take off your hiking boots so Mama can clean them." The girl sat on the sofa with a menagerie of stuffed animals.

After two days of staying close to home, she'd taken her daughter on their first outing, a short hike on a trail in town. Though she was worried that a hike would bring back bad memories for Elsie, her daughter had insisted that she wanted to pick some flowers and chase some butterflies. Being connected to nature was the most healing thing for her little girl.

Her rational mind told her that Norm, Sheryl and Gregory were all in jail and couldn't hurt them anymore. But that didn't make the fear of being out in the open from going away. Elsie's enthusiasm about getting to go outside had quelled much of her own fears. All the same, it was going to take a while for both of them to feel like things were back to normal. Though Elsie seemed okay, she knew there might be a delayed effect for what she had been through. She'd look into finding a counselor for both of them.

The whole time they were hiking, she'd been thinking of how nice it would be if River and Frankie were with them. Not just because of the sense of safety she felt when the officer and K-9 were close, but because she missed their company. Not having them around would be an adjustment after being in such close proximity. Elsie had asked several times if River and Frankie could come visit.

The child seemed to have bonded with both the dog and River. Lydia had answered that she didn't know. "River and Frankie have an important job to do."

While Elsie removed her boots, Lydia stared into an open cupboard, trying to decide what to make for lunch. She'd gotten a new stove, but the rest of the repairs would take some time. She really needed to go to the store. As much as Elsie would like to, they couldn't live on macaroni and cheese forever.

The doorbell rang.

Lydia ran ahead of her daughter. "Elsie, let me get it." She still felt protective of the three-year-old. Even letting Elsie out of her sight for a second or putting her down to sleep made her nervous. For sure, the healing over what had happened was going to take time. There was loss, too. She'd thought of Norm and Sheryl as family. They'd both been arrested and were awaiting trial for several crimes. Debbie had been devasted to learn about her parents and had promised to reconnect with Sloane. When she'd called Sloane to let him know Elsie was okay, he apologized saying he hoped that someday he could be in Elsie's life even though he knew he'd done too much damage for him and Lydia to get back together.

She opened the door. River stood with a pizza box in his hand and Frankie at his feet. He offered her a bright smile. "I thought you might be hungry."

Her heart fluttered as she looked into his blue eyes. Hadn't she just been thinking about him?

Behind her, Elsie jumped up and down. "Yeah, Frankie's here. Come on in, Frankie."

The dog wagged her tail then looked up at River. "Go, girl." Frankie bounded into the living room as Elsie laughed and danced around her.

He held the pizza toward Lydia. "So, are you hungry?"

How could he know that he had been on her mind so much? There was a bond between them that was about more than what they had been through together.

"Yes, actually."

They sat down at the table and ate.

Elsie finished her last bite of pizza. “Can Frankie and I go outside?”

Lydia glanced over at River. “Do you need to get going?”

“No. I cleared my day to come over here.” The look in his eyes, the warmth of his voice, made her want to melt. Something had shifted for him.

When they stepped outside, the spring sun warmed her skin. River and Lydia sat on lawn chairs, watching Elsie play with Frankie.

Her gaze wandered to the trees behind her house. Her breath caught when the memory surfaced of the attacker, who’d turned out to be Gregory, had run there.

River reached over, resting his hand on hers. “You and Elsie are safe now.”

“How could you tell I was thinking about that?”

He shrugged. “No one is going to hurt that little girl with Frankie around.”

“Yes, but you and Frankie—”

He leaned close to her. “Frankie and I would like to spend more time with you and Elsie.”

She turned to face him, searching his eyes, which filled with warm light. “What are you saying?”

“I want to be in your life. We need to give Elsie time to get used to me. You mean more to me than anyone ever has. Lydia, I want to marry you.”

Lydia let out a heavy breath. “Oh, River. Ever since you drove away, I haven’t been able to get you out of my head. It’s just an adjustment. I thought I would be raising Elsie alone. I just never thought I’d meet someone like you.”

“So, what do you say? We’ll make it a long engagement so Elsie can get used to the idea and I can get to know her better. Will you marry me?”

"Yes." She reached up to touch his cheek. He leaned in and kissed her.

Frankie and Elsie ran toward them, and she gathered them all into a hug, realizing that she had the family she had longed for since childhood.

* * * * *

If you enjoyed this story, don't miss
Danger in the Rockies,
the next book in the Colorado K-9 Unit series!

Discover all the books in
this brand-new continuity:

Searching for the Truth *by Laura Scott*
Tracking the Taken Child *by Sharon Dunn*
Danger in the Rockies *by Terri Reed*
Protecting the Baby *by Jodie Bailey*
Fugitive Manhunt *by Sharee Stover*
Hunting an Arsonist *by Jessica R. Patch*
Uncovering Explosive Secrets *by Maggie K. Black*
Unraveling a Crime Ring *by Valerie Hansen*
Christmas K-9 Security *by Lynette Eason & Lenora Worth*

Available only from Love Inspired Suspense!

Dear Reader,

I hope you enjoyed the exciting and dangerous adventure that Lydia and River went on to find little Elsie. I love that this book takes place in the spring in the Rocky Mountains of Colorado. Spring is a time of renewal after the dark and cold of winter. I chose the Bible verse at the beginning of this book from Song of Solomon because it talks about that seasonal shift. The image of flowers blooming and birds singing is one of hope and new possibilities. I feel like Lydia and River have gone through a dark winter emotionally when they first meet in the book. There's a shift they both need to make to let go of the past and open themselves up to the hope of love. We all go through dark and cold seasons. The good news is that we can look forward to a time when life blossoms with possibility and renewal. The winter does not last.

I love to hear from readers. You can learn more about me and my books and sign up for my newsletter at sharondunnbooks.net.

Sharon